Fallen
Short

Shedding Light On It All…

L. A. Lambert

ISBN: 978-0-615-44810-7

Published by L. A. Lambert, Philadelphia

Cover Design by D. Ink Graphics

Printed in the United States of America

I want to give special thanks to Monique Hester and Shakkie Clark for giving me the encouragement to make it over the biggest hurdle of this book, the First Chapter. Sometimes starting something is the hardest part in the process of completion. To one of the greatest men in my life, my father Tony Brown, thank you for showing me how one leap of faith can change your entire life for the better. Last but certainly not least, thanks to the other greatest man I know, Dr. Hayward Hamilton, for grooming me into the vessel I have become and taking time out to write the commentary at the end of this book.

This book is dedicated to my daughter, I promise to be the light you need to lead you on your path through life until your light is strong enough for you to walk on your own.

"No one lights a lamp and then covers it with a bowl or hides it under a bed. A lamp is placed on a stand, where its light can be seen by all who enter the house. For all that is secret will eventually be brought into the open, and everything that is concealed will be brought to light and made known to all. So pay attention to how you hear. To those who listen to my teaching, more understanding will be given. But for those who are not listening, even what they think they understand will be taken away from them."

Luke 8:16-18 (NLT)

Chapter One

(July 9, 2010)

They all sat around the long conference table staring at one another. There were six people gathered in the conference room. Each person's name was written on a place card in a strategic position at the table. Each had received a letter in the mail requesting their attendance at a very important meeting. Some of the guests were confused as to why they had been chosen to be there and some afraid to speak to one another for fear of giving up information from their past.

It was early afternoon on a Saturday in the middle of July. The sun was shining through the windows and generated an uncomfortable but bearable heat in the conference room. The silence was almost deafening as most of the attendees waited for what they believed to be closure to a life they cherished and would never forget. The sound of the conference room door opening broke the silence as the attorney entered the room and sat at the head of the table.

"Good morning. My name is Eli Whitley. Your presence has been requested here today to hear the reading of the final will and testament of Elizabeth Holden. If you would all please acknowledge your presence once I call out your name. Darnell Allen?"

A brown skinned man with an Italian tailored grey suit gestured his finger in the air. "Yes, I am here," he stated in a stern tone.

"Gabrielle Santos?"

"I'm Gabrielle," stated a young woman in a soft toned voice. She was seated beside Darnell Allen but had not looked at him from the moment she arrived.

"Trisha Johnson?"

"Yes, that's me." Trisha sat on the opposite side of the conference table across from Darnell and Gabrielle. Darnell stared with widened eyes at Trisha in amazement. He had not seen her in over fifteen years and did not recognize her.

"Malik Simms?"

"I'm Malik." Malik sat on the other side of Darnell. You could see the tension on his face. He did not look or speak to Darnell.

"Cynthia Holden."

"Yes I'm here." Cyndi's eyes were bloodshot red. She had not slept the past few nights. She could not believe her sister was gone. She was angry and sad at the same time and being in a room full of people from her sister's life did not help. As she looked around, there was one person whose presence calmed her down.

"Lily Woods"

Lily sat next to Cyndi and Trisha. She reached out and placed her hand on top of Cyndi's. "Yes, I'm here." One tear fell out the corner of Cyndi's eye. She looked up at the ceiling to fight the rest of the tears that were developing in her eyelids. It hurt Lily so much to see Cyndi struggle with her sister's death but she was glad they had gotten closure before she died.

"It looks like everyone is here" said Mr. Whitley. He opened up a folder that contained a small stack of envelopes and removed one of the envelopes that sat underneath. "Elizabeth requested that I read this letter before we proceed to the last will and testament."

The attorney opened up a business size white envelope and took out a handwritten letter. It had been embossed with Elizabeth's seal, a purple butterfly. "And it reads as follows, 'Each of you at this table has a confession written by me on your behalf. You have two choices, you can allow your confession to be read aloud in the midst of the present parties or you can choose to take your confession and forfeit what I have left you in my will. If you do choose to have the letter read aloud, you must remain through the entire reading of the will or you will also forfeit your rights to any possessions left to you. The choice is yours, but you must choose now."

The attorney refolded the letter and placed it back in its envelope. "I took the liberty of bringing the chest in today."

The attorney pointed to a beautiful hand-crafted lavender and gold chest that sat in the middle of the table. It was as long as a shoe box and had the distinct shape of an eyelid.

Malik shook his head in confusion. He had recognized the box but did not understand how it could've been the same box he had sold a few years ago.

There was a thick cloud of tension developing in the room. Mr. Whitley stood up slowly and raised his left hand in the air as to gesture for responses. No one responded. They all seemed to be deep in thought.

Mr. Whitley waited a few more moments and then placed the waivers on the table. "I do have a few other appointments today. So, if you will all please take a moment and decide if you would like to remain for the reading of the will or forfeit your inheritance. If you choose to leave, please be sure to sign this waiver."

He held a legal sized paper in his right hand, grabbed a pen off of the conference table and expressed, "This needs to be done now. Please understand that by signing this form, you are forfeiting your right of inheritance to Elizabeth's estate."

Chapter Two
Gabrielle
(September, 1987)

"I'm late for work! You need to hurry up!" Lydia yelled up the stairway.

She had been late to work for the past week and was in danger of loosing her job. Lydia was a stripper at a gentlemen's club in downtown Durham, North Carolina. She had been working there for the past four years and enjoyed her job, until recently. It had become burdensome trying to juggle school and work. Her boss was not very understanding to Lydia's needing to come in late a few nights a week, which added an even greater stress to her life. She was seriously considering getting a sugar daddy that could pay her bills while she went to school. Becoming a nurse was very important to her but what currently took precedence was getting to work on time.

"Hay Mamie you're going to make us late for work! You know how Mr. Johnson gets when we're late! I can't afford to have my pay docked tonight!" Lydia yelled up the stairs to her friend Liz.

"I am so sorry," Liz said as she ran down the steps. "I didn't know the church service I went to was going to be that long. It was awesome Lydia I think I'm going to become a Christian. I may have grown up in church but I can't honestly say I was ever a Christian. The preacher was talking about how God takes care of His children and you don't have any more worries or problems."

"Ok, well tonight you're going to be a bartender and I'm going to be a stripper. Can we talk about you being a saint in the car? I told you I need this money tonight. I have to pay for the balance of my class tomorrow and I still need three thousand dollars. I need every minute of pole action that I can get."

"If you became a Christian you wouldn't have to worry about that. Jesus would pay your bills!"

Lydia laughed as she grabbed Liz's chin, "Liz mamie, you always have this hope about you that scares me. You never believe you can't have something."

"And you never accept that there is so much more than what we have now. That's why we balance each other out."

As they pulled up to the strip club they could see the men lined up at the door to get in and could hear the music bumping from the walls.

"I'm taking an extra five percent of your tab tonight Lydia and I don't want no feedback." said Tony in a stern voice.

Tony Johnson was the owner of the strip club Lydia and Liz worked at. He handled everything from the music to the private shows at the club and was very stingy with sharing the profits. Lydia and Liz were only two minutes late but it was the point of him being able to dock their pay that mattered most.

"Tony it wasn't my fault! I was waiting for Liz and I really need the…"

"I don't care. And you can tell Liz she's getting docked tonight too and thank you for making ya both late!" Tony yelled back at Lydia as she stomped to the dressing room to get changed.

"You know you owe me Liz." Lydia snarled at Liz as she took off her sun dress to change into her outfit. "This class is very important to me. I only have two more semesters left and I'll be outta here. I'm finally doing something with my life. Why does he have to be so difficult? It was two stinking minutes and I don't even go on for another hour. I need a drink. I can't do this anymore, I'm going to quit right now. I'll get a sugar daddy…"

"Lydia, calm down girl your talking fifty miles per hour. I'll give you back whatever Tony docks you."

"Liz, you don't have to do that. I could of caught the bus here or had Hernando pick me up on his way to work. You have things to do too. Plus we gotta pay rent this week."

"Girl please shut up and take this money. I have my half of the rent already anyway. Don't worry about me. If I hadn't gone to that church revival, you would've been on time. It was worth being late though. The message was good and the preacher was fine! What more could a girl ask for!"

"A million dollars," Lydia mumbled under her breath.

"Any way, like I said, I got you. Just let me know how much you need to pay off that class of yours."

"Thanks Liz. I would love to know where you get all this extra money from but I won't pry."

The music stopped in the main room of the club as the mic was queued up. "We have a special treat coming up next for you. The lovely Luscious Lulu who's waiting to fulfill your fantasy."

"Guess I better finish getting ready. I'll see you out there Liz."

"Show them what your working with, but don't kill'em. You want them to come back for more!"

"Shut up Liz… go make my drink. I'm going to need it after this."

Lydia headed to the curtain to wait for her intro. She liked to watch the dancer that went on before her perform. It helped her gage how the crowd would be when she hit the stage. Each dancer got to pick her own song she would perform to each night. That night Lydia chose "Do You Want Me?" by Mishell Ndegeocello. As the song cued up, she drank both of her shots of Tequila and made her way to the stage.

As Lydia danced, a nice looking gentleman caught her eye. He was wearing a three piece custom tailored Armani suit. He was caramel brown complexion with a nice frame. As he sat down at a table near the main stage Lydia could see how handsome he was and became immediately turned on.

'Oh he's going to get a lap dance from me tonight!' Lydia thought in her head as she flipped herself in the air on the pole. She imagined they were the only two people in the room as she moved. Wrapping her legs around the pole with her feet in the air, she slowly slid down the pole using only her left arm for support. This made the man sit up on the edge of his seat. Lydia began to slowly glide up and down the pole exhibiting as much seduction as she could. As she moved she could see the man biting his bottom lip and licking his lips in timing with her up and down motion. Once the song was over Lydia plotted how she would get close to this new comer.

While the deejay introduced the next girl to perform, Lydia sashayed across the dining area trying her best to pretend the Italian suit man was not there. Teasingly she walked past him and went over to an older gentleman who was a regular on Wednesday nights. She gave him a lap dance for a minute and strolled seductively back towards the stage making sure to brush her right butt cheek on the man's shoulder. She then turned around and began walking towards him staring at a part of the wall right above his head so he would think she was looking at him. He began to smirk assuming Lydia was walking his way. He reached his hand out to grab her by the waist but retreated it once he realized she was not looking at him.

As Lydia walked past she waited five seconds before she turned around and whispered in his ear seductively. "You want me don't you?"

The man leaned in closer to Lydia and whispered back "I've already got you." He licked her earlobe as he leaned back in his seat.

Lydia's insides immediately became excited. 'He has no idea who he's dealing with!' Lydia said in her head. She had calculated she could get at least five hundred dollars from him. Lydia gestured for him to follow her to a private room. They walked to the red room where a security guard stood at the doorway.

The man whispered in her ear. "Can we go somewhere more private to than this? I'm in town for a few days. I'm staying at the Marriott downtown."

Lydia thought for a moment as she danced in front of the Armani suit wearing man. She had never seen this man before and how was she to know that he wasn't crazy and would rape her then leave her in a ditch on the side of the road. Her train of thought was broken by him reaching out and taking her by the hand. Lydia noticed the Rolex on his wrist and could not get the thought that he could pay off the rest of her semester.

He spoke in a deep sexy tone and said, "I don't want to hurt you unless you want me to." He then smiled at her and slowly released her hand from his all the while grinning and licking his lips at Lydia.

She leaned her head back to his left ear as she danced around him. "I don't know if you can handle me. I come with an expensive price tag."

"You name it, I've got it."

Lydia paused for a moment and then whispered in his ear, "Then yes. Meet me out front at three."

Lydia walked out the room and hid her excitement about her expected rendezvous. She had no idea who this man was but something about him intrigued her. She felt almost drawn to him. As if he had something she needed.

"He wasn't ready for this." Lydia said to the guard as she passed by him.

Three o'clock came around and Lydia was extremely excited to be picked up by her mystery guy. She had gotten so wrapped up in meeting him that she never asked his name.

Liz walked over to Lydia with her shoes and coat in her hand. "You ready? I cleaned the bar already so we can leave a little earlier tonight. Where are you goin?"

Liz was so focused on looking for her keys she hadn't noticed that Lydia was wearing a black sleeveless dress with her silver stilettos and silver accessories. She had even tied her hair up in a neat Chinese bun. "Lydia, I'm too tired to go to the diner. I'm sorry you got all dazzled up for nothing."

"Oh it's not for nothing, I've got a date."

"At three in the morning? I thought Hernando got off at seven?" Liz looked at Lydia in confusion.

"It's not Hernando. It's someone I met tonight." Lydia said with a sly smirk on her face.

A limo pulled up in front of Lydia and Liz. The front passenger rolled down the window and they were surprised to see that it was a woman "Which one of you is Lulu?"

"That would be I," said Lydia as she excitedly walked over to the rear door. "Don't wait up for me Liz!"

"And where exactly are you going?" Liz yelled in concern. "Can you give me a hotel name or something? What if this is a set up? You are so crazy Lydia…"

"Oh Liz, calm down! I'm going to the Marriott downtown! You can write down the license plate number if you're that concerned. I'll be okay, I'm a big girl." Lydia rolled the window up and the limousine pulled out of the parking lot of the club.

"Lord, please keep my crazy friend safe. She has no idea what she gets herself into half the time." Liz was shaking her head as she pulled out some paper to write the license plate number down.

Chapter Three

"I'm not going to work Liz. Just go ahead without me."

"Girl I think we should get you to a doctor! You've been sick like this for a week now. How much longer are you going to wait? Until you die?"

"You are so dramatic. There's been a virus on campus. Everybody in my class has been getting sick. I just need to rest. I've been running myself raggedy the past few weeks."

"Well, Monday, you're going to the clinic. Matter of fact, I'm going to make an appointment for both of us. If you've got a virus, I don't want to get it."

"Monday is three days away. I'll be better by then."

Liz grabbed her coat off the hook as she walked towards the front door. "Call me if you need anything. I'll keep the phone near me at the bar."

"Ok hun, Hernando took off tonight to come take care of me. I'll be better in no time."

Lydia jumped up from the love seat and ran to the bathroom.

Liz shook her head as she walked out the door, "Sure you will!" She yelled as she closed the door.

"Get up Lydia. Our appointments are at ten and eleven!" Liz was walking down the hall from her bedroom as she yelled into Lydia's doorway. It was now Monday and Lydia had not been able to hold food down for two weeks.

Lydia looked at the clock on her night stand. "Liz, its seven in the morning. Why are you up so early? The clinic is fifteen minutes from here." Lydia had buried her head under her pillows to avoid seeing sunlight. She peered her head out when she heard Liz yelling.

"I'm not trying to be in this clinic all day Lydia! If we get there early we might get out of there early."

Lydia pulled her covers up over her head and closed her eyes to go back to sleep. She yelled "Wake me up at nine please!"

Liz shook her head as she slammed the door to Lydia's room. "And you better get up!"

Liz walked into the kitchen and started pulling out pots and pans and loudly placing them on the counter top. She started humming the lyrics to 'This Little Light of Mine' and slamming cabinets as she took out the ingredients to make breakfast. She had just got the first few strips of bacon in the pan when she could hear Lydia getting out of bed. Liz smirked as Lydia's door slammed open and she stomped into the kitchen in her bath robe. She straightened her face out as she turned around to face Lydia. Lydia was standing right on her heels. "Why do you insist on waking me up? You do this all the time! Do you always have to get what you want?"

Liz scrunched her eyebrows in together as if she had an attitude. "All I was trying to do was cook us some breakfast! You know the walls are thin!" Liz attempted to hold back her smirk but it was no use.

"I knew you were trying to wake me up! You know I've been sick for almost two weeks and..."

Lydia ran off down the hall to the bathroom. The smell of bacon had turned her stomach completely inside out. Lydia thought of the last time she had eaten something solid and realized it had been three days earlier. She couldn't get her entire thought out of her head before she had to throw up again this time throwing up in the toilet as well as on her robe.

"Lucida Gonzalez." The doctor called out.

Lydia motioned her arm in the air as she walked toward the door where Dr. Moore stood.

"Ms Rodriguez, we did a series of tests to ensure we covered all basis. I'm glad to tell you that you do not have the flu. It would have been a very difficult few weeks for you and the baby."

"Baby? What baby. I think you're confused Dr. Moore. I don't have any children."

"I'm aware of that Ms Rodriguez; I was referring to your pregnancy. How far along are you?"

"I'm not far any where because I'm not pregnant!" Lydia grabbed her purse and stood up to head out the office door.

"I'm sorry Ms. Rodriguez, I thought you knew."

"No, I'm sorry that you're…" Lydia dropped her bag and ran to the bathroom to throw up once again. All she could think about as her head hung over the toilet bowl was, she couldn't even remember his name.

Liz slammed the bathroom door open and sat on the floor next to her best friend. "Lydia honey, it's going to be ok. I'll talk to Dr. Moore to see what you can take. You'll be feeling better in no time."

Lydia wiped her mouth on her sleeve. She sat down on the floor and started crying.

"Awe Ma, I know you hate throwing up." Liz stood up and grabbed a few paper towels from the dispenser and wet them with cold water from the sink. As she squeezed some of the water out of the towels Lydia blurted out, "I don't even remember his name!"

"Whose name?"

"I can't remember his name!"

"I can't believe I didn't use a condom! What was I thinking? I didn't even know him."

Lydia and Liz had been home for three hours and Lydia had been lying across the couch sobbing the entire time.

"We don't know for sure this is his baby. It could be Hernando's."

"No it couldn't. We haven't had sex in months. Since he switched his shift to take those classes I have hardly spent any real time with him."

"Oh Lydia! Well what can you remember about the man? Maybe we can back track and something will jog your memory."

"I remember his eyes. They were the most beautiful brown eyes. There was something about them that just drew me to him. It was almost like a trance. He said he was from out of town, Maryland I think. He had a conference he was doing in town. I remember this scar on his right thigh. He said his dad abused his mother growing up. He got fed up of them constantly fighting one night…"

"And grabbed a butcher knife out the kitchen to stab him?"

"How did you know Liz?"

"Remember that great preacher I told you about who was doing a revival in town a month ago?

"Yeah. What about him?"

"He told the same story. His mom grabbed the knife out of his hand and tried to stop him from getting involved…"

"And he fell on the knife. Liz, this can't be the same guy! The guy at the club had on this expensive Armani three piece suit. He couldn't have been anyone's preacher!"

"I can't believe I fell for his story! That's why I don't go to church now. I felt bad about not going to church like I said I was going to."

"This is crazy Liz. It can't be the same man! Preachers don't go to strip clubs!"

"Either this is the same guy or someone who has a very similar story."

Liz sat next to her and rubbed her back as she thought of how stupid she had been for believing she could change and how inspired she had been by the preacher's story. It made her sick to her stomach of how hypocritical he had been. She had been so convicted about the life she lived especially since she grew up going to church. Now she had no idea if church people were any better than she was.

"We're going to take care of this Lydia. We're going to take care of this." Liz said as she continued to rub Lydia's back.

The phone ringing broke the five minute sobbing session that Lydia and Liz had been having on their living room sofa. Liz reached over and picked up the cordless phone on the table behind their sofa.

"Hello." Liz said in between her sniffing. "Hernando! Hi. No nothings wrong, just a little under the weather." Liz's eyes widened.

"Yeah, I think Lydia might have given me what she has." Liz lied.

Lydia had jumped up in nervousness and immediately became nauseous again. She ran down the hall to the bathroom and slammed the door behind her. Liz cringed as she heard Lydia vomiting again.

"Hernando, Lydia's in the bathroom. I'll let her know you called when she gets out."

Liz slammed down the phone and placed the pillow from the couch over her head so she wouldn't have to hear Lydia throwing up.

Chapter Four

(April, 1988)

"Ok, Liz. You don't like Samantha, Carmelita or Marisol. What name do you like?" Lydia asked Liz.

Lydia was now seven months pregnant. She had decided to keep the baby after she attempted to go through with an abortion twice. She could not stand the thought of knowing she was killing another human being. She had just graduated from the nursing program and was two weeks away from taking the state exam. Hernando took the news about the baby hard but loved her too much to loose her. They got married when she was five month's pregnant and decided to put Hernando's name on the birth certificate.

Liz scooped another spoonful of ice cream out of her waffle cone as she and Lydia walked into Baby Gap at the local mall.

"Listen honey, this is your baby. You name it whatever you like. I'm just saying I wouldn't name my child any of those names!"

"Oh this is the most adorable sweat suit! Look at the little pink flowers on the bottom of the pants!" Liz said.

"You don't even know if this baby is a boy or a girl. You better get neutral color clothes like yellow and beige." Lydia started laughing out loud and the woman at the register stared at her as if to tell her she was being too loud.

"What is so funny?"

"I was thinking how funny it would be if you ended up having a boy and you had to bring him home in that violet dress you bought because you didn't have any boy clothes. That would be hilarious!"

"But you wouldn't let that happen would you? I know you'd find him something before he came home. What am I saying? I know it's a girl. I can feel it."

"Sure, just like you felt that you needed that second bowl of ice cream?" Liz started laughing uncontrollably.

"No, I can really feel it." Lydia yelled as she doubled over in pain.

"You're so dramatic!" Still laughing, Liz shook her head she had turned her back to Lydia and didn't notice she was doubled over leaning on the clothes rack

"Ma'am, are you alright?" the woman behind the counter yelled.

Liz turned around to see Lydia breathing heavily and a pool of fluid on the floor underneath her.

"Oh God! Someone call an ambulance! Her water broke." Lydia yelled as she put Liz's arm around her neck.

"It's too soon Liz! I can't have her yet! She's not ready!" Lydia said frantically. Liz was in tears as Lydia carried her over to a bench outside the store.

The woman behind the register ran out into the hall. "I called the police, someone's on the way."

"Liz we gotta pray! I can't loose my baby! This can't be happening!" Lydia was sobbing and panting at the same time as she and Liz sat in the hall of the mall waiting for an ambulance to arrive. Liz realized she didn't know how to pray. She didn't know if God would even hear her. She had to do something though, so she obliged her friend's requests.

"Dear God, please don't let Lydia loose this baby. Please send your angel Gabriel to keep Lydia and her baby. We believe on you to keep her and her baby. We have faith that you can do miracles and we're asking that you do one for her right now." Liz said as she began to cry as well. She felt this warmth come over her as she prayed for Lydia and her baby. She hadn't felt that in a very long time and somehow she knew that everything would be okay.

The mall security ran down the hall toward them with the paramedics following close behind. Lydia grabbed Liz's hand as she tried her best to breathe calmly. "Gabriel, I like that name. If it's a girl, I'll call her Gabrielle."

Liz smiled at Lydia and squeezed her hand back. "I like the sound of that. And when they grow up, we'll tell them that they were named after the angel that protected them." Liz closed her eyes and held on to Lydia's hand to fight back her own tears. She thought in her head, if God never did anything else in her life she would still be eternally grateful to him for protecting and keeping Lydia's baby.

Chapter Five
Trisha
(August 1988)

"Shannon, I cannot keep doing this," Trisha whispered into the phone. She had been assigned to be the administrator for a prominent preacher, Reverend Darnell Allen, who held conferences up and down the east coast. She also worked as his PR and troubleshooter when he enjoyed himself too much after his revival services. Trisha knew how to keep the strippers he slept with quiet and discreet. She would also report back to his father, Bishop James Allen, all of his son's indiscretions. Trisha had been a member under the leadership of Bishop Allen since she was a child. She had also been friends for years with Darnell's wife Shannon. Trisha tried her best to convince Shannon that her husband was being faithful and she bought it, until recently.

"Trish, I know this is hard for you but imagine how I feel. I'm stuck at home raising our three kids while my husband is out doing God knows who and not even thinking twice about how this affects our family or his father's ministry!"

"I have to go. I think I hear him coming down the hall." Trisha hung the phone up and turned the volume up on the television. She began laughing in cue with the audience on the television show. Darnell walked into the room and plopped down on the love seat next to Trisha.

"I know you were on the phone. What did my wife want this time?"

"She was just checking to see if you had come straight to the hotel after you preached tonight or if you had one of your rendezvous again."

"You know, sometimes I wish she would just leave me! If I didn't love her so much and we didn't have the kids I would leave her."

"Darnell, she has every right to feel the way she does. I mean lets face it; you were a dog when she met you but she loved you beyond your faults. She just believed that having children would make you change."

"Humph is that what she thought. I love those kids and I want to set a good example for them. That's why I would never sleep with anyone that lived in the Atlanta area. I would die if one of those chicken heads came to my house or called my wife."

"Darnell, you're mess is going to catch up to you one day. And if you think answering to God for it is something; you haven't seen the wrath of Shannon Allen."

Trisha gets up from the love seat and heads toward her suite. Darnell grabs her wrist and Trisha turns toward him.

"What Darnell." Trisha says in an annoyed voice.

"You know I can stop anytime I feel like it."

"Yeah, well, I would love to believe that but…"

The door bell to the suite rings and there is pounding at the door. Darnell mutes the television and puts his right pointer finger on his lips as if to signal Trisha to be quiet. Trisha rolls her eyes and yanks her arm out of Darnell's hand. She heads to the door and is quickly followed by Darnell who speeds his pace up and beats Trisha to the door. He looks out the peep hole and turns his back to the door again signaling Trisha to be quiet.

"I know you're in there. I need to talk to you!" A woman yells on the other side of the door. "I can hear you at the door. I'm not going anywhere." The woman's voice shakes as if she is crying.

Trish yells out, "Who are you?" Darnell covers her mouth to stop her from continuing to speak.

The woman's eyes pop open wide and her mouth slightly drops.

"I'm so sorry. I thought this was Reverend Allen's room. I do apologize for disturbing you. Please forgive me." The woman begins to walk away from the suite door. Trisha bites Darnell's hand and begins to speak once again.

"This is his suite," Trisha yells from behind the door. She manages to get the door open while Darnell was checking his hand. Trisha looks down the hall and is shocked to see a woman turn around with a huge stomach.

"Do I know you ma'am? You look familiar." the pregnant woman says.

"If you're looking for Reverend Allen then yes, I'm his assistant." Trisha turns around and points her hand inside the hotel suite only to see that Darnell has disappeared.

"I'm sorry ma'am. I never caught your name."

"It's Kim. I'm sorry if I'm disturbing you. I really needed to talk to Reverend Allen. Is he here?"

"Yes he is but unfortunately he's unavailable to speak at the moment." Trisha said in a coy voice. Darnell stood behind the door breathing a sigh of relief.

"But if there is something I can help you with, I'd be more than happy to do so. I handle all of Reverend Allen affairs and I do mean all of them!"

"I'm not sure I should be addressing this with you. I really need to speak to Darnell I mean Reverend Allen myself." Kim responded.

"Trust me ma'am, there is nothing you could say that would shock me." Trisha said.

"I don't know ma'am. What is your name any way?"

"Trisha. Listen ma'am I don't mean any harm but he is not going to speak with you so if this is truly an important matter, your best bet would be to talk to me."

The woman stared at Trisha for a long time and began to burst into tears. She grabbed Trisha by the neck and began to wale on her shoulder. Darnell took this as his cue to run into the bedroom and lock the door.

"I'm pregnant!" The woman yelled.

Trisha stood back for a moment and looked at the woman's stomach and said as if she was confirming it, "Yes you are."

"Darnell's the father."

"Oh no I'm not!" Darnell yelled from the bedroom as he opened the door. "Woman you must have the wrong man. Try one of the other men you slept with. I always and I do mean always strap up before I go into the jungle."

Trisha glared at Darnell and shook her head while rolling her eyes. "Darnell please spare me!"

"I'm not here to ask you for anything. I just thought you should know. I heard on the radio you were back in town so I just decided to take a chance and see you."

"What do you want woman? If you're not asking for anything, why are you here?"

"Because you deserve the right to know you're going to have a son!"

"I can't believe this. You really think I'm your baby's father? The last thing I remember is you leaving this nasty note in my suit pocket telling me if I came back to town I would have you to deal with. Now I'm supposed to believe that I'm the father of your child? " Darnell's voice shook slightly as he repeated back in his head what was happening. He zoned out of the conversation and went back to the three nights he had spent with Kim. Darnell day dreamed about that last night and couldn't remember if he had actually used a condom. He was so lost in his own thoughts that he had not noticed the woman began to bend over in pain until he felt a splatter on the bottom of his pants. "Did you just spit on me?" Darnell looked down to see a small puddle on the floor between the woman's legs. "Awe hell no!"

Trisha nudged Darnell on the arm pushing him back into the room. "Call an ambulance Darnell! I think her water just broke."

The woman was now down on her knees in the doorway of the suite. Trisha bent down to grab Kim by the arm and helped her into the suite.

"She's fine just where she is." Darnell yells from the living area of the suite. Trisha continues to help the woman into the suite ignoring what Darnell is saying.

Darnell sensing he had been thrown out of the way obliges with Trisha's request and calls the front desk to have an ambulance sent.

"Trish what's the room number?"

"1215. Tell them to hurry!"

"1215. Thank you."

Darnell hung up the phone and began pacing back and forth across the living area. On his fourth pace the phone rang again. Darnell quickly grabbed for the receiver assuming it was the front desk. "Are they here?"

"Is who here? Darnell what are you talking about?" Shannon said.

"Hey baby! Sorry I thought you were the front desk."

"What's going on? Why do I hear a woman screaming in the background?"

"Sweetie I'm going to have to call you back. A woman went into labor in the hallway. I'm waiting on the ambulance to come get her. I'll call you back."

"Darnell don't play no games with me! What's going on? Where's Trish at?"

Darnell pointed the phone towards Trisha who looked confused. Trisha stopped wiping Kim's brow with a hand towel she took out of the bathroom and grabbed the phone from Darnell. "Shannon I really can't talk right now. There's a woman that's about to have a baby. Her water broke and we're waiting on an ambulance."

Before Shannon could respond Trisha hung up the phone.

"I cannot believe this! I cannot believe this! Woman tell me the truth. Is this my baby?"

"Yes!" Kim yelled at Darnell. "I, I, I have to push!"

"Oh no you don't! Trish close her legs! The ambulance isn't here!"

"Shut up Darnell! She can't stop the baby from coming its too late for that! If yall had used protection in the first place we wouldn't be dealing with this!"

There was a knock at the door and Darnell ran to open it. The paramedics rushed in with a stretcher. "We got a call that a woman was in labor."

"Right in here sir"

"I have to push." Kim said between breaths.

"Ma'am please don't push yet. We need to get you on the stretcher." The first paramedic said as he attempted to take her pulse.

"I don't think she's going to make it. She's completely dilated and 100 percent effaced." The second paramedic said.

"Ma'am I need you to continue your breathing like you're doing. That's great. I know you want to push and you're in a lot of pain but I need you to just hold off for a few minutes while we prep everything."

"Please tell me you're not going to do this right here! Oh Lord! Ok. This is not happening." Darnell said.

"I can't do this with him here! Darnell just go! I only told you I was pregnant because I thought you would want to know about your son! I don't want anything from you! Just leave!"

Darnell stopped and looked at the whole situation in front of him and broke down crying on his knees. "God, what have I done?"

As he knelt with his head down, Trisha came over and slapped Darnell on the back of the head. "Snap out of it Darnell! You can talk to God later; this baby is coming right now."

Trisha grabbed Darnell under his arm to stand him up and dragged him over to Kim. "Darnell I can't do this right now!"

Darnell reached over and grabbed Kim's hand. "I'm sorry Kim. Let's deliver this baby and go from there."

Kim could see the sincerity in Darnell's face as he knelt down on the floor beside her.

Chapter Six

It had been three years since the hotel room incident and things had only gotten more complicated since then. Trisha drove up to the drive way to the suburban home of one of Darnell's former lover's. She hesitated before she hit the buzzer on the outside gate. This was the third time she had to do this but it did not make it any easier. She shook her head and pushed the buzzer. A female answered on the intercom. "Who is it?" The voice said.

"My name's Trisha. I spoke with you on the phone." Trisha heard a buzzer and waited for the metal gate to open. She drove up the driveway to a cul-de-sac and parked in front of the doors to a brick front home. She got out of her jaguar and held the envelope she had in her hand tightly. As she walked up to the door she said a quick prayer. "God please help me not to judge your children. Give me a heart of compassion and not condescension."

Trisha opened her eyes and rang the door bell. A few moments later the door was slightly opened and a woman peeped out. "Hi I'm Trisha John..." Trisha was cut off by the woman closing the door on her. She bowed her head and began to pray again, "God bridle my tongue Lord. Please, Jesus help me to hold my peace." She lifted her head to see the door open and a well dressed black woman standing there with her hand on her hip.

"Trisha Johnson I presume?" The woman said as she leaned back on the door and put her arm out to welcome Trisha into the house.

"Yes, I'm Mr. Allen's attorney." Trisha stood in the doorway a little confused since she thought she was there to see a Hispanic woman.

"Lydia is inside." The woman said.

Trisha walked into the house and was amazed at how nice it looked. She had imagined a tacky house with a bunch of beads hanging in the doorways, cheap furniture and a bunch of baby toys in the floor. Instead she saw a well kept home with a gourmet kitchen and marble floors. There was a chandelier in the middle of the dining room that resembled a French design she had seen in a magazine. As Trisha stared at the chandelier a woman walked up beside her.

"I saw this in Modern Home magazine and I just had to have it."

Trisha turned to see a beautiful Hispanic well dressed woman standing beside her. Trisha reached out her hand to shake the woman's hand and the woman reached back. "Hello, I'm Trisha Johnson. I spoke to you a few days ago."

"And I'm Lucida. Yes, I remember who you are. I'm sure you might not recall me however. I bet you're thinking I cleaned up pretty good." Lydia said with a sarcastic undertone.

"Ma'am no disrespect but you were not what I expected. I know it's been a few years but I... Please forgive me."

"It is fine. Now to the reason you're here."

"Yes, I know you said you did not want anything to do with Mr. Allen but he has requested that I reach out to you. Believe it or not, I kept a very thorough record of his encounters with the opposite sex and I had no choice but to follow up with you. We had a private investigator check into the last five years of your life and…"

"Ms Johnson…"

"Please call me Trisha."

"Trisha, I know Mr. Allen is my daughter's father. I don't want anything from him, our daughter is enough and as you can see I have made a very good life for the both of us. I don't want or need anything from him. My husband and I make a pretty good living so I am not in want for anything."

"I completely understand Mrs. Santos. However; Mr. Allen would like to be sure he takes financial responsibility for his part in this whole situation. I brought a letter for you to sign to have a confirmation that you agree to a blood test being done. Once the results come back, if they reveal Mr. Allen is the father of your daughter, you will be sent a check in the mail for twenty four thousand dollars which will cover the past two years of a one thousand dollar stipend Mr. Allen has agreed to pay every month."

"You are not understanding me ma'am. We're talking about a little girl not a situation! Her name is Gabrielle. She's not some prize. I appreciate Mr. Allen trying to do the right thing now but I don't even know how you got in contact with me or even knew I had a daughter. This is too much right now. I just buried my mother not too long go and this is just too much!" Lucida got up from the couch she was seated on and walked out of the room into the kitchen. Liz, who had been standing in the doorway during the conversation walked into the room never taking her eyes off of Trisha and sat on the couch next to Lydia.

"Do you have any idea what Lydia has been through? She didn't even know she was pregnant. Then to have to deal with the reality of having to explain to her daughter one day that she was the product of a one night stand! On top of all of that, she marries her childhood sweetheart who accepts her daughter as his own. They have been through years of counseling to get past this and now you bring it all to the forefront!

"Ma'am, please do not think I am trying to be cold but don't you think this little girl…"

"Her name is Gabrielle."

"Yes, don't you think Gabrielle deserves to know that her father, her real father cares enough to make sure she is taken care of?"

"You call this taking care of a child? Excuse me for sounding frank but money does not make you a care provider. Listen Trish, I don't want to go back and forth with you and as you can see, Lydia does not wish to speak with you any more. If you just leave the paperwork, I'll talk to her. Does she have a way to contact you?"

"Yes, my office number is on the bottom of the letter and here is my business card. Please have Mrs. Santos contact me when she is ready."

"I will do that" Liz snatched the papers out of Trisha's hands. She placed them on the coffee table and stood up to walk Trisha to the door.

"Also thank her for agreeing to see me. I appreciate her taking the time out to meet with me." Trisha tried to express as much empathy through her words as she could.

"I'll let her know." Liz had turned her back to Trisha and was holding the front door open.

Trisha walked towards the foyer and noticed a picture of a beautiful little girl sitting on the mantle in front of a mirror. She sighed a deep breath and let herself out of the house.

Chapter Seven

As Trisha opened the door to her hotel suite, the phone on the night stand next to the bed rang. Her head was pounding from the days events. She wondered how someone could put a price on a life as if it was an object. How do you decide what's enough and what's too much? It made her sick to her stomach to believe that she had actually suggested Shannon go behind her husband's back and pay off the mothers of his illegitimate children.

'What makes it so bad is that Darnell believes his wife has no idea about these other children! I can't take this anymore! I'm spending too much time trying to cover up and protect these ungrateful self-centered people! No one ever thinks about what is important to me! Put Trisha on this plane to go here and take care of this because I need this done today. Is it too much to check and see what I might be doing with my own life? I can't do it! I'm done!'

Trisha was yelling at the top of her lungs and had started crying uncontrollably. She noticed that she had pulled out some of her hair in her frustration. Trisha held her hands on her ears as she balled up in the corner of the living area of her suite rocking back and forth and sobbing. The whole time in the background she heard the phone faintly ringing.

A few hours later Trisha woke up with a splitting headache on the floor in her suite. She picked up the phone in the room and called the front desk. "Yes, can you have a van pick me up to take me to Durham airport? I'm not sure what time my flight leaves. I just want to leave as soon as possible. No sir, I don't want to check out early. Yes. I understand but I just need to go to the airport to book my flight. That would be great if you could do that for me. Yes, I need the first flight tomorrow afternoon to Atlanta, Georgia. Thank you, I appreciate it. Oh, one more thing. Please take a message if I receive any calls. I do not want to be disturbed for the rest of the evening."

Trisha hung up the receiver. She looked up at the ceiling in her room for a few minutes wondering what her life would be like if no one knew she existed. She let out a deep sigh and rolled onto her stomach to pick herself up off the floor. Just as she made it to her feet, her room phone rang.

'I thought I told him no calls.' Trisha thought as she shook her head. She reached over and picked the receiver up off the hook.

"Who is it?" she yelled. "Bishop Allen, I'm sorry, how did you know where I was staying?" Trisha said in a confused tone.

"Trisha, Stephen called me. I know what Shannon put you up to. He's very concerned about you and I'm concerned about your marriage. Come home and take care of your family. This has been going on long enough without me interfering. Darnell and Shannon need to sort out their own marriage. I'm sorry I let this situation get this far. Take a few weeks to get yourself together and the four of us will have a meeting,. I've prayed about it and it is time I release you. I'm removing you as my son's administrator.

When he stopped following the will of God was when you should have come to me. I understand your loyalty to your assignment but God has a greater use for you than being involved in this mess."

Trisha began crying on the phone uncontrollably. She thought she had cried every tear she could a few hours earlier but there were more tears buried deep down inside.

"You have a husband and a son to think about. I can't afford to watch two marriages fall apart because of one person's issues. I've talked to Stephen, he has arranged for you two to take a trip to California to my beach house. Stephen Jr. will stay at the house with Lady Allen and I while you're away. We'll be sure he gets to school and is taken care of."

"Thank you Bishop. I…"

"Hush child, pack your things and let your husband know when you're at the airport."

Shannon hung the phone up and felt like she had a huge burden lifted off of her. She had become so entangled in Darnell's mess that she lost all conviction for helping him feed his cravings for women. If she didn't do what was asked of her, no matter what it was, she felt she was not being accountable to her assignment. After the past few situations, she had become burdened with being torn between feeling guilty about covering for Darnell and wanting to live her own life for fear of appearing to not be committed to the ministry. She loved God and her church but had become burned out trying to keep up with her own life and her assignment. On top of that, she had to split loyalty between her best friend and her best friend's husband which had made her become cold toward them both. What it boiled down to was that she had become so consumed with making everyone happy that she never realized how unhappy that made her.

Shannon fell back on her bed about to doze off again when the room phone rang.

"Hello. Yes, what time is the flight? Ok, please have a car pick me up at two thirty to take me to the airport. Thank you."

Trisha pushed the button to hang up the call. She dialed the number to her house. Her husband picked up.

"Steve, it's me."

"Hey honey. Are you alright? You sound like you've been crying."

"Yes, I'm fine, just a little tired. How's Junior? Tell him I'm sorry I missed his game again. I promise I won't miss another."

"He's good. They won the game, but you know in peewee football both teams win." Steve chuckled lightly on the phone. His voice changed as he continued to speak to his wife.

"Baby, did Bishop call you?"

"Yes, I just spoke to him not too long ago. My flight leaves tomorrow at four so I should be back by five thirty."

"Honey listen, I don't want you to think I was trying to go behind your back and speak with Bishop but someone had to do something. Trish I've never seen you so drained before. You're my wife and I love you. I couldn't watch you slowly disappear in front of my eyes. When you're home, you're not here and when you're gone you're definitely not here."

"Steve, I understand. Thank you. You don't know how much I love you."

"I love you too honey. So you said your flight gets in at five thirty? We can stay at the airport and take the red eye to San Diego. Would that be okay?"

"Sure if you knew how to pack for me! The last time we took a trip you only packed underwear, bras and tube socks for me. I had to buy a whole new wardrobe just for the trip."

"Maybe that was all I wanted to see you in."

"Shut up Steve, you're so fresh."

"Only when I'm talking to you."

"That better be the only time you talk like this!"

"I miss you baby."

"I miss you too."

"No, I really miss you. I miss us."

"Steve, I know. I'll make it up to you and Junior also."

"Junior's a kid, he's too young to understand anything."

"I know but I don't want to wait until he's too old to make it up to him. You're my two favorite men."

"Honey get some rest. I'll meet you at the airport and I'll be sure to pack more than underwear and bras. I'll put a toothbrush and deodorant in the bag too!"

Trisha laughed as she shook her head at her husband. Until that moment, she didn't realize how much she really missed just laughing with him. "I'll see you tomorrow. Kiss Junior for me and tell him I will see him soon."

"I will. Good night baby."

"Good night Steve."

Trisha hadn't realized how late it was. She had been back at the hotel since three. It was almost ten o'clock. She jumped up, packed her bags. She figured if she did everything tonight, all she had to do in the morning was wash and put her clothes on. Trisha ran some bath water as she picked her outfit for the next day's journey. She played the radio clock in her room while she took her bath to calm her down. After she got out the tub she read a few chapters of Proverbs before she went to bed. It was a new day even though it was evening and Trisha was excited about the changes that were taking place. She went to sleep with the thought that it was time for her morning, night had lasted long enough. She needed her joy back.

Chapter Eight

Cynthia

(June, 1990)

Cyndi staggered up the street until she got to the entrance of The Ritz Carlton in downtown Detroit. She smirked as she thought back to when she was a child and dreamed of living in a hotel like this. She leaned against the revolving door and fell as the door began to move under her left arm. The doorman rushed over to help her up while she was still attempting to lean on the moving door. Cyndi slapped his hand away as she was trying to help her self up and pushed the door to even more. The revolving door slid past the point of return and Cyndi's feet got caught between the door and the round window that cased it. She fell into an uproar of laughter as she shimmied her feet to get them inside the door. Finally releasing her feet, Cyndi crawled on the floor while the revolving door continued to turn until she was able to crawl inside the building. The doorman immediately attempted to help Cyndi to her feet again as she continued to laugh uncontrollably. "I am so sorry Madam, are you okay?" Cyndi quieted herself and looked at the doorman with the straightest face she could make. Instead of responding to him, she burped loudly in his face and covered her mouth as she ran towards the restrooms.

"I shouldn't have drunk that last shot of tequila. What do you always tell yourself Cyndi? Ten is enough!" Cyndi was scolding herself in the mirror of the ladies room in the lobby of the hotel. Cyndi stood up straight and pointed her finger as she stared at her reflection. "Now get yourself together! This is no way for a Holden woman to act! We have an image to uphold! You have to uphold the family legacy and name!" Cyndi burst into laughter again and dragged herself out of the ladies room.

In the lobby of The Ritz, the manager stood waiting at the front desk with his arms folded tightly across his chest. Cyndi straightened up upon seeing him and walked as soberly as she could to the front desk. "Madam, are you a guest with us this evening?" The manager asked with a straight look on his face.

"Sir, I am Elizabeth Holden. I lost the key to my suite, would you be so kind as to give me another?"

"I'm sorry but I do not believe I'll be able to do that."

"And why is that sir?" Cyndi questioned in a pompous tone.

"Because I believe your key has been found."

"Well that's very interesting. And who exactly found it?"

"I did." A woman in a knee length black dress and Jimmy Choo black pumps emerged from the elevator. "Apparently I checked myself into this hotel a few days ago after I mysteriously thought I lost my wallet. I was only reminded when I called my credit card company to find out I had checked into this hotel in Detroit. The strangest thing is I made the phone call to the credit card company in my home, in Georgia!"

"Hi sis! I didn't expect to see you here! How's the hubby and the little one?"

"Cyndi don't even try it!" Liz walked over and stood toe to toe with her sister in law.

"Would you like us to call the police Mrs. Holden?" The manager said as he walked to Liz's side.

"Oh, no thank you Pierre. That will not be necessary. I think I can handle this from here." Liz said, never taking an eye off of her sister in law.

"Sir, I would like for you to call the police. Please!" Cyndi grabbed the manager's arm and pleaded with him.

Liz pulled Cyndi's arm off of the manager and dragged her towards the elevator. "Shut up Cyndi! I can't believe you! I thought you were going to stay sober!"

The two women got on the elevator and Liz smiled at the manager as the doors closed. As soon as the elevator began to lift she turned to Cyndi and began yelling. "The penthouse suite Cyndi? The penthouse suite? How drunk are you anyway? You reek of alcohol! Why the hell did you steal my wallet anyway? Do you know how much grief you've caused me? I don't understand why you continue to do this to yourself let alone your family!"

"Just tell me you didn't tell my brother! He doesn't need to know about this with him being sick and all."

"Is that all you're worried about? I can't believe this! You know if he wasn't getting worse I would've told him as soon as I got off the phone with the credit card company!"

"Whew! I love you Liz. Thank you so much for keeping him out of this! The last thing I want to do is..."

"The last thing you want to do is what? Get yourself together? You know you are the only other person I have besides your brother and Victoria? We practically grew up like sisters! If something happens..." Liz began to cry uncontrollably as the elevator doors opened to the penthouse suite on the twentieth floor. She calmed herself down enough to stop crying. "You will be all Victoria and I have left if something was to happen to Charles and I can't live with you being a mess like this around your niece. So if you can't get yourself together then, then." Liz began to cry again. She had been trying to avoid giving Cyndi this ultimatum for the longest and hated that things had come to this point. "Then I will have to pretend you do not exist. I'll explain everything that has been happening to Charles, tell him about your recent relapse and hope that he will understand and agree with my wishes."

"Liz! Okay, I know I messed up but I didn't mean for it to go this far. I'm sorry about the wallet. I just figured you'd cancel the cards out eventually and just count it as a loss. Since I used up my trust I didn't have any other way to get money."

"You used up your trust! That was five million dollars Cyndi! God! What is wrong with you?."

"I had a very hard time dealing with my mom dying. I know its been five years but it feels like I was just talking to her yesterday." Cyndi had begun to cry out of empathy and threw herself on Liz.

Liz pushed Cyndi off of her back onto the love seat. "Just stop it Cyndi! Please, just stop it! You were a drunk way before your mother died! The excuses are getting old! Your trust ran out because it ran out! You had the choice of investing it but you chose to quit your job! You chose to go on those elaborate trips for years! You chose to drink your life away. No one else did this to you but you! You also had the choice to come back and run the foundation. Cyndi please don't make me have this conversation with you." Liz was yelling by this time and had tears rolling down her face. She calmed herself down again and began to speak in a softer voice. Cyndi had lain across the love seat trying to hold her head up so that Liz knew she was paying attention. "Cyndi, this was the last straw. I know I've said this before but this is it. You get yourself together or I don't want to see you again and I don't want you around my family."

"They're my family too." Cyndi said in a sarcastic tone.

"If you continue to act like this, no Cyndi, they're not your family. You are no longer welcome in my home."

"That's my parent's house! You were just the nanny's daughter who grew up in a trailer home. You're not even worthy to use the bathroom in that house!"

Liz slapped Cyndi in the face. "How dare you! How dare you get indignant with me! I loved you like you were my own sister. And yes I lived in the trailer but who came running to the trailer when her parent's were too busy to be bothered with her? Whose mother took you in when your own mother turned her back on you? You have no right! I have never been snobbish towards you and I will NOT accept this! I worked hard for everything that I've gotten and I will not have you insult me! I love your brother mansion or trailer home!"

"I'm so sorry Liz. I'm drunk! I don't know what I'm saying. Please forgive me. I, I, I'm such an idiot."

"Get yourself together and be ready to check out in the morning. You're on your own after that! I've got a plane to catch."

Liz grabbed her coat and bag and headed toward the elevator. She turned back around as she waited for the doors to open and said with tears running down her face, "I love you Cyndi."

As Liz got on the elevator Cyndi wallowed in her own tears on the love seat and contemplated committing suicide. She rolled herself off the couch and began to stomp around the living area yelling at herself at the top of her lungs until she became nauseous. She had never seen Liz like this before and wished she had thought things through a lot more thoroughly before she stole her wallet.

Chapter Nine

(October, 2008)

It had been ten years since Cyndi had seen Liz. Cyndi had voluntarily enrolled herself into a rehab center in Augusta, Georgia and had been sober for two weeks. She ran down the hall panicking because she was late for her afternoon group counseling session Cyndi caught her breath before she walked into the door. As she checked her watch she realized she was only a few minutes late and didn't think it was a big deal.

"If you're going to take your rehabilitation seriously you had better start being on time," the counselor said.

"I'm sorry, I had fallen asleep reading a book and I…"

"And I don't really care. Have a seat." Lily Woods was a woman in her early thirties. She was a therapist with specialized training in drug rehabilitation. She had a brother who she condemned for being a chronic alcoholic. After he died she had a first hand experience of how hard it was to quit when she herself had become an alcoholic. Lily had found herself drunk, stumbling into a church over fifteen years ago. The pastor prayed for her and she instantly became sober. She dedicated her life to Christ that day and won the battle over alcoholism. Lily carrying the burden of never being able to ask for forgiveness from her brother before he died made her even the more passionate about the AA meetings she counseled. Lily was very serious about each person who had chosen to change their life by remaining sober and only allowed a person to be late twice before kicking them out of the meetings.

Cyndi sat in the empty chair next to Lily and kept her eyes to the ground shaking her right leg. She was having a hard time fighting the urge to drink and shaking her legs seemed to calm her nerves. Lily placed her hand on Cyndi's leg to stop it from shaking as she took her seat.

"Now, who's next?" Lily asked.

"I'll go." said Cyndi.

"But you have no idea what today's exercise is."

"Ok, what is the exercise?"

"Toni, how about you go next. Cyndi, you can go after Toni."

A five foot four petite woman stood up and closed her eyes. She was silent for a moment before she began to talk about what happened the last time she had a drink. She confessed that she had been so angry that she had beaten her five year old son to the point that he started bleeding. Her son laid on the floor as still as he could in fear that if he moved she would continue beating him. Once she realized what she had done, she went to the bathroom and tried to cut her wrists with a razor. She had passed out on the floor and woke up in the hospital a few days later. The doctors told her she had almost died of alcohol poisoning. She began to weep as she told everyone that she was so drunk she couldn't even commit suicide right. Her husband had been gone for over two weeks. She had no money for food and the lights were going to be cut off the next day. The only thing she could think to do was drink. This had been over three years ago. Toni sat down and looked at Lily as if to receive some type of consolation for the way she felt at that present moment. Lily looked at Toni and said, "I need you to remember the way you feel right now every time you think about taking a drink. This is the lowest you can get Toni. You can only go up from here."

"I think I'm ready to go now," Cyndi said.

Cyndi stood up and closed her eyes to go back to ten years earlier. "I had just found out my brother had died and I was completely devastated. My parents died when I was nineteen. My brother and his family were all I had left. I had been sober for a year and I was doing great. I was helping my sister in law take care of my brother. He was diagnosed with liver cancer when he was thirty and we thought it was in remission until he got sick again out of no where. When he died I felt betrayed. He was supposed to hold on. He was a fighter. I went to the wine cellar in my parent's home and drank until I couldn't drink anymore. I left the house and went to a bar in town where I drank some more. The last thing I remembered was riding the car onto the side walk and running over something. I panicked and drove off down the street out of town. I ended up pulling off the road somewhere outside of town to sleep in the back seat of the car. When I woke up I drove back to the house to learn that my niece had died in an accident the night before. Apparently a drunk driver had driven onto the sidewalk and ran her over as she was coming out of the pharmacy. It wasn't until a week later that I realized I had hit her with the car. Once my sister in law realized it was me, she pointed a gun at my head and told me she never wanted to see me again and that I was dead to her. That was ten years ago. It didn't affect me until two weeks ago when I was walking down the street and saw an article in the newspaper about a foundation for the families of victims who died from hit and runs. It was the Victoria Holden Foundation, named after my niece. I never thought about the long term effect something like that could have on the family until then and it was my own family." Cyndi put her head down and cried for a moment. She took a deep breathe before she began speaking again. "The hardest part is knowing that the last time Liz saw me I was messed up. I'm here for her and because of her and even if she never sees me sober, I have no choice but to stay sober. My drinking has destroyed enough lives."

Lily took Cyndi's hand as she sat down. "That is why it's so important that you take this seriously. I know how important this is to you but you have to control yourself even more now than you have ever done before. You're in a fight and any moment you're not winning, you're losing. There's no such thing as trying, only doing."

"I know Lily, you're right. No one wants to hear me trying; they want to see me doing."

Cyndi spent the remainder of the session thinking of what her life would've been like had she never started drinking. Lily clasped her hands together breaking Cyndi out of her trance.

"Ok, I think that's enough for today. Thank you all for sharing with us today. It is a great step in your progress to be able to face who you use to be. I will see you all tomorrow, the same time."

As everyone walked out of the room, Lily called out to Cyndi. "I wanted to speak with you for a moment Cyndi."

"Yes."

"Do you really believe Liz won't want to see you again? If you'd like I can talk to her for you. I know she needs you just as much as you need her right now. She's upset and it's understandable; but she can't stay angry forever."

"Lily, you don't know her like I do. I've never seen her act like this. She was going to blow my brains out. The crazy thing was that I was going to let her. I deserved to die."

"I don't want you to beat yourself up about this. You are taking steps to be a better person and that will be seen."

Cyndi shook her head as she walked away from Lily. All the grief and depression she fought hard to keep from feeling came rushing over her. She rushed down the hall to her room and ran to the bathroom. Throwing up seemed to become a daily event in the past few weeks for Cyndi. She sat on the floor in the bathroom leaning on the toilet crying. She hadn't felt so alone in her life. She heard foot steps coming towards the bathroom and quickly grabbed some toilet paper to wipe her eyes and mouth.

She heard a light tapping on the door and looked up to see Lily standing in the doorway. Lily walked over and sat on the floor next to Cyndi. She wrapped her arm around her shoulder. "I know that this is supposed to be hard but I can't do this alone Lily."

"You're not alone Cyndi. Have you ever prayed before?"

Cyndi looked at Lily with disdain in her eyes. "Lily, no offense but God is the last person I want to talk to right now. I'm going to hell anyway so what would He want to hear from me for?"

"Cyndi, God is the first person you need to talk to! You are not alone. Because you're still here means God cares. You're his child Cyndi he loves you. Now, you have a chance to live a life with Christ by your side. He's been there for you the whole time. You just never knew it."

"I don't understand Lily. I've never heard him or seen him. This is ridiculous you don't know what you're talking about!"

"The story you told the group earlier about the last time you were drunk. Remember how much you said you drank? There are not many people that can drink that much and not die, let alone drive a car and survive! God is watching out for you whether you want him to or not."

Cyndi had begun to yell and cry at the same time. "Did he watch my brother die? What about Liz? Did he watch her suffer while she buried her husband and her daughter? Did he Lily? Answer me!"

Lily wrapped her arms around Cyndi as tight as she could and held on to her with all her might. She quietly prayed that God would give her peace so that she could get through the hurt she was feeling and learn to forgive herself. They sat on the floor of the bathroom that way for three hours. Not speaking a word to each other.

Chapter Ten

For the first time in almost fifteen years, Cyndi did not have the urge to drink. She had a bad headache from all the crying she had done the day before. As she lay in the bed she thought about the conversation she had with Lily the night before. She tried to word her mouth to speak and for the first time couldn't quite get the words out. A tear rolled out the corner of her right eye as she realized for the first time in her life she was afraid to speak. She licked her lips and opened her mouth. The only thing that came out was a sigh. Cyndi sat up in the bed and looked at her legs under the covers. "How did I get here?" she asked out loud. "God, how did I get here?" She began to cry again and stopped herself abruptly. "What am I doing? What am I doing? I need to get up and get myself together." As she sat up on the side of her bed, she saw a box wrapped in red wrapping paper sitting on her night stand. She opened it and found a Bible inside. A yellow piece of paper stuck out of a page. She opened the Bible to that page and saw it was a card that read 'You're not alone! Love, Lily' She grinned slightly and started reading the Bible.

"Okay group. Today I want you to take some time and write a list of everyone you've done wrong to because of your addiction. This is a very important step to not only complete the process of rehabilitation but also to free you of any guilt that may remind you of what you use to be. Please bring this list with you next week. I'm going to go through strategies of how to approach these people." Lily stood up and began to pack her things into her backpack when Cyndi walked up to her.

"I've already made my list and since most of the people on it are gone and the one person I can reach out to refuses to hear from me, where does that leave me?"

"Cyndi, it's been ten years. Time heals all wounds. You never know what to expect if you reach out to them."

"I took her child's life, she'll never forgive me."

"The question is; will you ever forgive yourself? You cannot expect anyone to truly be able to forgive you if they can see you haven't forgiven yourself. The point of this is not to get someone to show you pity but to gain their forgiveness. Time heals all wounds Cyndi, so let it heal yours."

"I understand you Lily. How do I do that?"

"I don't have an answer to that Cyndi. Only you can figure that out." Lily picked up her bag and left the room. Cyndi sat down in one of the chairs in the circle and stared at another empty chair. All she could think about was her brother's birthday that was coming up in a few weeks and how she couldn't believe he was gone. Cyndi sat in the chair for hours thinking about her life up to this moment. What had she accomplished? What did she have to be proud of? What could she offer anyone? The answer she came up with was nothing.

"Mrs. Holden, you have a call." Liz's assistant said over the intercom for her office phone.

"Who is it?"

"Lily Woods. She said it's about Cynthia?"

Liz's heart began pounding in her chest. She had not heard from Cynthia in almost ten years. "Put her through."

Liz reached her hand out to pick up the phone. She stopped short of picking it up and took a deep breath. "This is Elizabeth Holden."

"Hi Mrs. Holden, my name is Lily Woods. I'm a counselor at the Shady Oaks Rehabilitation facility. You're sister in law Cynthia has been a patient here for about six weeks. Were you aware of that?"

"No I wasn't aware of that. Is there something wrong? Is there an issue with the payments?"

"Ah, no ma'am. There isn't an issue with the payments. It's actually Cynthia I was calling about."

"Oh dear Lord, please don't tell me something happened! I don't think I can take any more bad news right now!"

"Ma'am no, it's not that. She's okay physically. It's her mental state I'm concerned about."

"I'm not sure I understand. Is there something wrong or is there not something wrong?"

"Yes and no."

"If its money she needs I can have my secretary draft up a check for whatever the amount is. I wouldn't want her to cause any problems at your facility. Other than that I am not sure how I can help you."

"Cynthia is doing very well. She's been sober for six weeks and she has opened up in the group sessions. She has made tremendous progress since she first got here. There's only one thing that seems to be holding her back from completing rehab."

"Well what is it?"

There was silence on the phone for what seemed like ten minutes. "Hello? Hello? Ms. Woods are you there?"

"Yes, I'm here. I don't mean to intrude Mrs. Holden. It's just that you're the only thing holding up Cynthia from complete recovery."

Liz placed the receiver on her shoulder as she stared at her computer screen. She could feel her temples pulsating. 'How dare this woman who has never met me and doesn't know anything about my relationship with Cyndi call me and blame me for Cyndi's issues.' Liz thought as she shook her head. She immediately started to get a sharp pain in both of her temples. She began breathing deeply hoping it would calm the tone of her voice before she spoke.

"Exactly who do you think you are? You have no idea the hell Cyndi has put me through! Do you know how much she has taken from me? My child is dead because of her. I had to bury my husband, her only sibling by myself and mourn the loss of my child! And what did Cyndi do? What she always does, drown the days away in alcohol. I have tried over and over again to help her, to reach out to her, to be her savior, friend. Why am I talking to you about this? Like I said, you have no idea!" Liz could not fight the tears back. She had not spoken with anyone about how she had been feeling. It felt as if a weight had been lifted. She was also embarrassed to have gone off on the poor woman on the phone. "I'm sorry. I just. What is the problem with Cynthia?"

"I can relate to how you feel Mrs. Holden."

"Please, I do not like being patronized."

"Liz, I had a brother who was a drug addict. He almost completely ruined my entire life. My career was ruined because of him, my husband left me because I spent more time bailing my brother out of situation after situation and not enough time at home. I became so bitter that I told him one day I was through. I completely disconnected myself from him. The problem is that I was the only person he had left and instead of me just stop being his enabler, I stopped being his sister. If I ever regretted anything in my life, it was the day I cut my brother off. I found out a few months later that he had died in a car accident. He wasn't the drunk driver, someone else was. I never got the opportunity to tell him he was forgiven. I'm a Christian woman and I didn't have compassion on my own family."

"I'm sorry to hear about your loss. I hear what you are saying and I appreciate you telling me that story but I don't know if my heart can take Cynthia disappointing me again."

"All I'm asking is that you come see her. She told me you are the reason that she has fought to stay sober. She doesn't want to let you down anymore. Even if you never see her sober, she still is convinced that she is not just sober for herself but for you as well. She carries so much guilt that I'm afraid she will never stay sober. Please Liz, just one day. You don't even have to speak. You can just listen."

"I'm sorry but I can't. I'm not going to allow myself to get pulled in. She made her choice years ago and she chose alcohol over me."

"I really wish you would reconsider Liz. Trust me, you don't want to wake up one morning feeling guilty that you didn't reach out to Cynthia and she's gone."

There was silence again on the phone. Liz missed Cynthia. She couldn't lie about that to herself. She just couldn't bring herself to fall back into that place of enabling her again. It felt like that's all Cynthia wanted her around for. Liz also remembered the vow she had made to her husband to take care of Cynthia. Liz pulled her calendar out from her desk drawer searching for a day that she could say she didn't have time. Almost instantly a warm feeling came over her body. It was a peace that she had not felt in a long time. She heard something whisper softly to her saying, 'Go, not later but today. Your sister needs you. I'll be the strength you both need.'

"I have to go." Liz said as she fought back the tears. She hung up the phone before Lily could say good bye. Liz became overwhelmed with a presence she had never felt before. Part of the message Bishop Allen had preached that Sunday, The God of the Sweep Through, came to mind.

"When we decided to change some things in our lives, we used what God gave us; our hands, to pick up and remove the mess our bad choices left behind. When we look back, all that we say is the debris or the emotional wounds and scars that developed in the transition. Instead of leaving our mess where it was, we dragged it into the next bad choice we made. Our heart has become broken and we find it hard to completely love and forgive again. But because God loves us so much, He became our broom and sweeps up the broken parts of our heart that had fallen along the way. He takes those broken parts and uses the living water to wet it and mold your heart back to how he created it to be, whole. Only God has the strength to not try to reshape something that was fine the way it was. So let the Lord sweep through your life and reshape your emotions, your mind and your heart."

"God I hear you. I just don't know how to let go of this pain. It's been ten years and I still miss my husband and my daughter. I miss Cynthia but I'm just so angry and hurt and enraged when I think about everything she's ruined in my life! I've tried letting her back into my life so many times before and I've just been disappointed. Help me to not fall apart. Help me to be a better person in her life. I need you Lord."

Liz had never prayed like that before. It was not as extravagant as her usual prayers but it was honest. She felt another weight fall off of her as she lay on the floor in her office. She didn't want to move from where she was. She couldn't move from where she was. Liz laid there until she felt that she had the strength to not only forgive Cynthia, but also help Cynthia forgive herself.

Chapter Eleven

Lily sat in her office reading her bible. She was still on edge about the conversation she had a few days earlier with Cynthia's sister in law. There was a degree of anger in her voice that she knew too well. Lily had prayed after Liz hung the phone up. She asked God to help her get over her grief and anger. Lily shook her head remembering too well when she felt that same way. Her thoughts were disturbed by a tapping on her door. A woman stood in her doorway.

"Are you Lily Woods?"

"Yes I am. How can I help you?"

"I spoke with you on the phone a few days ago about my sister, Cynthia."

Lily's eyebrows scrunched in confusion.

"I know you weren't expecting to see me but I have done a lot of thinking and praying and well here I am."

Lily smiled and stood up from her desk. "You're Liz?"

"Yes I am. I'm not sure when visiting hours are but I do want to see Cynthia if that's ok."

"Yes, yes it is." Lily said as she nodded her head. "Actually we are about to have our afternoon meeting. If you'd like, you can come with me. Today we are going through our list of people we've hurt and family is allowed to come in and listen. You came on the right day."

"I'm not sure I'm ready for that. I just wanted to say hello and maybe talk another time."

"Today is the day. You're here for a reason Liz. You can sit in the back."

Lily walked over and led Liz out of the doorway down the hall to the meeting room. Lily froze up at the door. "I can't. I just can't"

"I won't pressure you. We'll be in here for an hour. There is a general reception area down the hall. You can wait there if you'd like until we are done."

"Okay, I can do that. Thank you." Liz turned around and began to slowly walk down the hall. She could hear Lily talking to the group as she walked into the meeting room.

"Okay everyone. Please find a partner and take out your lists."

Liz had made it halfway down the hallway and stopped herself. "What am I doing? I asked God to give me strength so I should believe that He'll give me strength!" She turned back around and walked down the hallway. She heard Lily telling everyone to partner up as she peaked in the doorway, she saw Cynthia standing alone. Liz stood in the doorway of the room and waited for Cynthia to see her.

Once everyone else in the room had a partner, Cynthia stood alone. Liz walked up to Cyndi and said, "You'll partner with me." Cyndi turned around to see her sister in law Liz standing in the doorway. She automatically felt overwhelmingly emotional but did her best to maintain her exposure.

"How did you know I was here? I thought I had lost you forever! I don't know what to say. I…I…"

"We can talk afterwards." Liz said in a calm voice. Her hands were shaking and her heart was beating rapidly. She took a few deep breaths to calm herself down. As she breathed she felt herself calming down.

Lily stood in front of the group and put her hands up to get everyone's attention. "Ok. I would like everyone to look at the list I asked you to write last week. I want you to take the name of the first person and portray that person to your partner. You're partner will play you. I want you to say everything that you believe the person you are making amends with will say to your partner."

Cyndi turned and faced Liz with a solemn look on her face. "I'm the first person on my list Liz."

"Then I think it's time you make amends."

Cyndi closed her eyes as the tears fell down the corners of her face. She began to think about everything that had ever gone wrong in her life and was almost overwhelmed with emotion. "I'm sorry."

"Is that all you have to say? You took time to come talk to me and all you can say is I'm sorry?" said Liz

"I didn't go anywhere, you came here. Liz…" Cyndi said in between tears.

"My name is Cyndi. Or did you forget that?" Liz snidely asked.

Cyndi almost forgot that Liz was portraying her and was about to leave when Liz grabbed her hands."

"Why are you sorry?" Liz's voice changed to one of compassion.

Cyndi hesitated and closed her eyes trying to find the words to say. "I've spent decades burying you inside of me. I thought if I drank, I wouldn't have to deal with how much of a failure I was."

"I never said you were a failure."

"But I knew I was. From fifteen on I have spent so much time trying to bury every mistake I've made that got me to where I am now. I was wrong though. I thought the alcohol would somehow numb me to all the pain I felt. I… I…" more tears began to roll down Cyndi's face. She wasn't ready to let go of the biggest secret she had kept most of her life. She closed her eyes again and went back to that day twenty five years ago.

"Let it go Cyndi."

"How could I let them take you away from me? You were mine"

"What was yours?"

"I thought they were doing what was best for both of us. I didn't want to be an embarrassment to the family. So I let them take you. I never even got to hold you. I never named you. Just gone, you were just gone. I went home like it never happened." Cyndi did not open her eyes while she spoke.

"What Cyndi? What are you talking about?" Liz yelled. By this point the rest of the members had turned away from their partners and were looking at Cyndi and Liz.

"My baby! How could my mother do that to me? She told me I wouldn't ever have to think about the baby again but I have. Everyday for the past twenty five years, I thought about it. How it looked. What color its hair was. I wondered if it favored me or not. I've been so ashamed for abandoning my baby. We just left the baby in that cabin. Like nothing ever happened. She said I would forget! Why can't I forget? I'm sorry. I'm so sorry. When I went back to check to see if the baby were still alive, it was gone."

"Cyndi, why didn't you tell me?" Liz grabbed Cyndi and hugged her as tightly as she could. "I forgive you for you. Now you need to forgive yourself. It wasn't you're fault. You were only fifteen. It wasn't your fault sweetie. Let it go Cyndi. Let it go."

Everyone in the group was crying along with both of them. Lily walked over and placed her hands on both Cyndi and Liz's back. "I think it's time that both of you forgive." Lily said.

A few hours later, Cyndi and Liz sat in the dorm room on the bed facing each other. "So when I found out I was pregnant, momma made me swear to never tell anyone. When I didn't return from Christmas break that year it was because I was in my last trimester. I was being homeschooled and Momma had sent me to Portugal to stay with one of my relatives until it was time to have the baby. I went into labor early and ended up having the baby at the cabin in the back of the house. I snuck back to the cabin a few days after I delivered the baby and it was gone. I didn't know what I would expect when I went in that cabin but I had to go. We got on a plane a week later and I finished out the school year like nothing ever happened."

"We were best friends, why didn't you ever tell me?"

"I didn't want to think about what had happened. I never even knew if the baby was a boy or a girl." Cyndi shook her head and lifted her eyes to look at Liz. "I want you to know I'm really sorry for everything. I've taken more from you than should be taken away from any person. I let my addiction take over me and I've lost so much because of it."

"Cyndi, I forgave you a long time ago. I just couldn't see you if you were going to stay the way you were. It hurt me too much to see you wasting your life away."

"I love you Liz. And I promise this is it. I can't spend another day pretending I don't have a disease. I believe God will heal me of it but I have to have faith that He will."

"Look at you! Somebody's been doing some reading!"

"Yes! Lily gave me this Bible a year ago and I've been studying everything I read. I'm really changing Liz"

"That I can believe! I love you Cyndi."

Liz and Cyndi talked until visiting hours were over and when Cyndi went to sleep that night, she felt a peace that she hadn't felt in decades.

Chapter Twelve

Darnell

(September, 1987)

"If you are ready to let the Lord into your heart and surrender your all over to Him, meet me at the alter." Reverend Allen stepped down off of the pulpit at a tent revival in Durham, North Carolina. As he walked toward the alter area created, he pulled a bottle of Pompeian Extra Virgin Olive Oil out of his robe pocket and took the top off. As people began to line up in the front of the church he would trace a cross symbol with the oil on each persons head. There were fifteen people lined across the alter as Darnell backed up toward the pulpit behind him to grab the microphone.

"Everyone gather hands as we pray for these souls tonight. I need everyone to pray along with me. Father we thank you for these lost sheep returning back home. We ask that you forgive them of their sins Lord. Wash them in the blood of your precious lamb. Jesus you gave your life that we might be able to have salvation. These children come to you now Lord to learn what they must do to be saved and we thank you for the opportunity you're giving them to receive salvation tonight."

Reverend Allen placed the oil on the wooden table in front of the pulpit that read, 'This Do In Remembrance of Me' across the front of it. He walked over to a woman in her mid twenties who looked as if she had been crying the whole message and gave her a hug. The woman lost all composure and fell back into the arms of a nurse. As she lay on the ground, Reverend Allen turned to the other fourteen people who had gathered at the alter.

"Each of you stands here because you have decided to accept Jesus Christ as your Lord and savior. I want you to lift your hands and repeat after me. "Jesus, I accept you into my heart. I believe that you are the Son of God and you died on the cross for my sins and in three days rose again." The fourteen people standing people with their hands raised repeated after Reverend Allen. He continued, "Jesus come into my life and make me whole."

The nurse helped the woman who had fallen out back to her feet. She had her repeat the steps to salvation. The woman lifted her hands as high in the air as she could and yelled out, "Thank you Jesus!"

"Fifteen more of God's children have accepted salvation tonight. That's something to praise God for!" said Reverend Allen

"Hallelujah!" the woman yelled and fell to her knees to weep. Reverend Allen came over and patted her on the shoulder. He walked away after a few moments and left the tent to go into the church.

The pastor of the church, Bishop Ortes, picked up the microphone and dismissed the service. When Reverend Allen returned to the tent to greet the people, the woman he had prayed for was sitting in a chair speaking to one of the ushers. She spotted Reverend Allen as he was looking her way and got his attention. Reverend Allen walked towards the woman and noticed how attractive she was. He quickly reverted his focus from her breast once he got close enough for the woman to notice. The woman reached out her hand to shake Reverend Allen's hand and he opened up his arms to hug her. "God bless you Reverend," The woman said as she hugged the Reverend back. "God bless you sister. I am so excited for what the Lord is about to do in your life. You took a very important step tonight!"

"Yes, and I'm excited. I feel like I can take on the world now!"

"Well, take your walk of salvation one day at a time, sister..."

"My name's Elizabeth Holden but my friends call me Liz. It's a shame this is your last night in town. I would've brought my roommate with me had I known that. I'll be sure to bring her the next time you're in town."

The usher whom Liz had been speaking to walked up beside Liz and put her hand on her shoulder. "You know you can always bring your friend with you to bible study or prayer or even Sunday worship. We're here to encourage you Sister Liz."

"Thank you Mother Johnson! I appreciate that," Liz said.

"You know, Mother Johnson is right. It is very important to stay connected to a church and Ebenezer Baptist is a great church. I've been holding tent revivals here for three years and before that, my father, Bishop Allen, was coming here for fifteen years." Reverend Allen said.

"I'll definitely be here on Sunday morning. Good night." Liz picked up her Gucci pocketbook and her jacket as she left the tent toward the parking lot.

Reverend Allen turned to Mother Johnson and put his hand on her shoulder, "Have you seen, Sister Johnson?"

"I'm right here Reverend." Trisha said as she walked toward the two from the parking lot.

"Sister Johnson, if all matters have been settled, I would like to head to the hotel to get some rest." Reverend Allen said.

"Oh we can have one of the deacons take you back to the hotel. It won't be any trouble." Mother Johnson said.

"No, that's fine; I have a driver waiting for me in the parking lot. I just wanted to make sure Sister Johnson had a way to the hotel. Are you ready Sister Johnson?"

"Yes, just let me grab my things out of the office."

"Ok, I will be at the car."

Reverend Allen said his goodbyes to the remainder of the saints in the church and walked to the town car waiting for him in the parking lot. He scouted out the lot to see if Liz was still around so that he could continue to talk to her but it was too dark to tell. Just as he sat down in the back of the town car, Trisha opened the front passenger door.

"I'm sorry; Mother Johnson was talking to me about getting you to come back next month or something? Did she mention anything to you? I'm so tired I don't know if I said good night to her."

"No, she didn't mention anything about that. Can you call and make sure the limo is waiting for us at the hotel?"

"What do you mean us? Aren't you tired? You've been preaching for the past four nights! You should be winded by now!"

"I haven't gone out yet since we've been here. I wanted to make sure I didn't hinder God from moving like He wanted to! I deserve to have fun one night!"

"If you want to have fun you can go home to your wife!"

"Oh come on Trish, don't start that! She knows I'm a man. I can stop anytime I feel like it!"

"What ever Darnell, how long have you been saying that? Three years now! Give me a break!"

"Just make sure you confirm the limo! You don't have to go with me anyway, you know that!"

"That's not the point Darnell; it's the fact that YOU don't have to go! I'll confirm the limo." Trisha grabs the mobile phone from column the of the car. "Hello, this is Trisha Johnson. I need to check if a limo has arrived yet for... Ok, thank you. Good bye."

Trisha slams the phone back on the hook and stares out the windshield of the car.

"Well, is the limo there or no?" Darnell asked in an agitated voice.

"Your limo awaits sir." Trisha replied in a snide tone.

Darnell reached out and placed his hand on Trisha's shoulder and said in a much softer and condescending tone, "You'll never understand the pressure I'm under. You think I want to be like this? Everyday I fight..."

"Don't feed me the bull Darnell. The only thing you fight is how long you're going to keep your penis in your pants!" Trisha pushed Darnell's hand off of her shoulder and got out of the car.

Darnell immediately got out of the car and quickly walked over to Trisha attempting to avoid a scene. He gripped her arm underneath her elbow and moved in closely to the right side of her body. "You will respect me and my position. I will not tolerate you speaking to me anyway you please. I am still a man of God and you will respect that." Darnell let her arm go and spoke in a softer tone. "You're going to get back into that car, remove the nasty look on your face and fix your attitude. You have no right to speak out of turn to me. I know we're friends but you will not disregard my authority."

Darnell watched Trisha as she got back into the car and stood outside for a few moments to calm himself down. He felt guilty and horrible for the way he treated Trisha. It was more of the fact that she was right than the way she spoke to him. How could he correct her for telling him the truth? He used their closeness to make her feel as guilty as he did about the entire situation. He didn't want to put Trisha in this situation but felt that her loyalty to him was the security that he needed to continue to sleep around on his wife. Darnell's disgust quickly disappeared once he saw Liz run pass him in a rush. He immediately became very aroused by watching her legs as she ran to her car. Darnell shook his head to try and shake the thoughts he was having but they would not suppress. Darnell got back in the car and waited for Trisha to look at him through the rear view mirror. "Can you call the hotel and find out the closest club near there?"

Chapter Thirteen

"Shannon, have you seen my red and yellow tie? I can't find it anywhere. I wanted to wear it this weekend at the revival in Harrisburg."

"Did you look in your travel bag where you're other ties are?"

Darnell walked over to the suit case opened on the bench in front of their oversized king canopy bed. He looked through the suit case frantically, "I don't see it in the suit case Babe. Are you sure it's in there?"

"No, I'm sure it's not in there."

"Okay Shannon, I don't have time for this! I don't want to get on the road too late."

"It's not in your suitcase because I told you to look in the travel bag; which is on the floor next to your suitcase." Shannon pushed Darnell's leg out of the way to reach for the bag on the left hand side of the bed. She placed it on the bed and began to look through it. She retrieved the tie, threw it on top of the suit case and turned to walk out the room. She made it to the doorway and turned around. "You're welcome." She said as she smiled at Darnell.

"Get back here woman!" Shannon turned and ran out the bedroom door laughing as she ran down the long hall toward the steps.

"You think you're just so slick." Darnell said as he chased after Shannon down the hall with the tie in his hand.

"I learned it from the master!" Shannon thought Darnell had stopped chasing her and turned around right into him. Darnell had a sneaky smirk on his face and wrap the skinny red and yellow tie around Shannon's back and pulled her close to him. Shannon wrapped her arms around Darnell's neck and began to passionately kiss him. A single tear fell from her left eye and landed on Darnell's cheek. "I'm going to miss you this weekend. You should let the kids and I come with you. I'm sure it wouldn't be a problem. I can get a replacement teacher for Sunday school."

"Babe, you know I would love for you and the kids to come with me but I would rather not have you leave so abruptly. How about you come to the revival in St. Louis a few weeks from now? I'll arrange everything now so it won't be so last minute."

"I need you Darnell. Besides, the kids start school in a few weeks. I don't want them to miss any days if they don't have to."

"Well, I can get my mom to stay with the kids. I'm sure her and Bishop would enjoy that."

"I guess that will have to do. It will give you and I chance to catch up."

Darnell began to get turned on by the words his wife spoke. He pulled her in even closer to him and began passionately kissing Shannon again. "What time does my flight leave again?"

"You still have at least five hours."

"And where are the kids?"

"Still at the park with my sister. They shouldn't be back until after you leave. You know how hard it is on them every time you leave."

"And what are you doing right now?" Darnell asked as he grabbed Shannon's butt and squeezed it tightly.

"Anything you like."

"I love you woman." Shannon gave Darnell such a feeling of love and contentment when he was with her. The problem arose when he would have to be on the road for weeks at a time. It caused Darnell's eyes to wander and eventually so would the rest of his body.

Darnell took the tie from around Shannon's waist and stood behind her gently guiding her back to their bedroom. He focused on the moments he had with Shannon because presently they were few and far between. "I'm going to miss you too Babe. Just let me enjoy this time I have with you."

Four Days Later

"And let the church say Amen! I would like to say that God has moved mightily these past three nights leading up to tonight and He has truly moved like never before tonight! I am so blessed that Christian Cathedral allowed me to come and preach what thus saith the Lord."

The congregation began clapping and giving praise to God. Darnell looked in the audience and was shocked to see his wife standing in the back clapping along with everyone else. He quickly cut his eye to a woman in the front pew who was clapping as well and immediately put his eyes back on his wife. The woman in the front turned while she was clapping to find out what had made Reverend Allen's facial expression change so quickly.

"I want to thank God for my lovely wife surprising me by coming out tonight. Baby stand up so everyone can see how beautiful you are!" The woman in the front stopped clapping and held a face of disgust as she grabbed her belongings and stormed out of the church. Shannon watched the woman's face as she stormed past her. Darnell continued speaking into the mic as if the whole event did not occur. "Honey, why don't you come up here and sing a few bars of my favorite song?"

Shannon put her hand up to signal that she didn't want to sing trying to hide the look of disgust that she felt at that moment. She mouthed the words next time as she smiled at the congregation.

"She said next time. I'm sure she's tired from the flight. I am going to turn the service back into the hands of Deacon Bridges at this time to give the benediction."

Darnell was still in shock that his wife showed up out of the blue. The woman in the front of the church had been staying in his suite the past two nights and his heart was beating three times faster than normal when he thought of what would happen at his hotel suite when they got back. He quickly looked over to his left to get Trisha's attention. Trisha looked at Darnell and quickly turned her attention back to Shannon. Darnell made a hand signal her way and Trisha looked at him. He mouthed to her to go to the hotel and Trisha's eyebrows quickly raised as her eyes got big as if she had not remembered the woman was staying with Darnell. Trisha blinked her eyes and slightly nodded her head as to not draw attention to herself.

Chapter Fourteen

(Following Service)

"I'm pleasantly surprised to see you baby. I thought you were going to come to St. Louis in a couple of weeks. Either way I'm glad you're here." Darnell nervously chuckled and turned his head to look out the window of the town car taking them to the hotel. "You know the funniest thing happened before service tonight. I was…"

"Honey who was the woman that stormed out of the church during service tonight? She looked as if she had just been slapped in the face. Did I miss something?" Shannon smiled at her husband and waited for him to turn his head away from the window.

"Oh, it was nothing. She had been trying to speak with me all weekend and I guess it was more than a church related conversation that she wanted to have." Darnell stared into his wife's eyes and did not blink until she turned her eyes away from him. Shannon put her head down and looked at the wedding band on her hand. "Are you sure that's all it was? There's nothing you need to tell me?"

"Honey, what would make you ask me that?"

"It was the way she looked at me when she walked past me as if she had a problem or something."

"I think you're reading too much into it."

"Are you sure?"

"Honey, yes. I don't know this woman besides seeing her at the revival services."

"Hmm, interesting. Ok, just figured I would ask."

Darnell quickly thought of a topic to lighten the air. "So when did you get in anyway. Are you just staying for the day? I didn't see the driver bring any bags to the car."

"My flight got in around five. I went to the hotel, dropped my stuff off in the room and headed to service in the cab."

"Awe honey you didn't have to get your own room. You should've let Trisha know you were coming if you wanted to surprise me."

"Funny you should mention that. I didn't reserve a room, I just asked the desk clerk for a key to your room. I showed him my id and he gave me the key."

"You, you went to my room?"

"What's wrong Darnell? You're sweating and you look a little pale. If you're worried about me seeing that other woman's clothes and stuff don't worry, I didn't throw them out. I neatly folded them and placed them at the door with a note."

Darnell's face became flush as a million thoughts ran through his head.

"Do you want to know what the note said?" Shannon smirked as she watched how nervous her husband had become. "The note said, 'Leave my husband alone and this will be then end of it. If you don't, you'll have to answer to me. Love, Shannon Allen."

"Honey I'm sorry. It just happened this one time. She doesn't mean anything."

"I'm just glad that the clothes didn't belong to the woman at the service. That would've been a shame, she looked so upset already."

"Yeah, you're right honey. That would've been a shame…"

"Darnell cut the crap! Here's what you're going to do. When we get to the hotel you're going to check out. We're going back home and you're going to get your act together. We're going through counseling and I'm telling you now Darnell, cross me again and I will make you're life a living hell. I'll be at every revival service. Every time you have to pee, I'll be there to zip your pants up."

At The Airport the Following Morning

"Flight 263 to Washington, D.C. is now boarding. Please report to the gate with your boarding passes and identification available."

"Baby, I'm really sorry. I promise I'm going to change."

"Just prove it to me. I don't want to hear anything else about it. Just prove it."

Darnell reached in his pocket to get his drivers license out of his wallet and found a note folded up inside of his wallet. He quickly took out his card and tucked the wallet into his jacket pocket. Once they boarded the plane, Darnell immediately went to the bathroom and pulled the note back out of his pocket.

'Darnell, I can't believe you never told me you were married! I am so disgusted with myself for letting you use me and my body as if my feelings weren't important. I really thought we would have a chance to get to know each other better! How dare you let me give myself to you and make me think what we had was special? You call yourself a Reverend? I would spit on

you if I was standing in your face! I hope you NEVER think about returning to Harrisburg again because if you do, you'll have me to deal with!

Darnell folded the letter back up, ripped it into pieces and threw it in the garbage. He had decided it was time to focus on his family and marriage and stop sleeping with other women. Before leaving the bathroom, Darnell prayed that God would help him to be the husband he knows he can be. "I cannot believe this happened to me! How could I be so stupid letting that woman stay in my room? God, what is happening to me? I'm slipping. I can't loose my wife!"

Darnell walked back to his seat and put his hand on his wife's. She pulled her hand out from under his and turned her back to him. He reached his hand up to put it on the small of her back and changed his mind. They spent the rest of the flight in silence only speaking to the flight attendant when necessary.

Chapter Fifteen
Malik
(May, 2006)

Malik ran down the hall to his dorm room almost knocking three people over on the way to the door. He banged on the door and yelled to his roommate who was still sleep. "Craig open the door! I forgot my key! Hurry up man! I left my final project on my desk." He banged some more and began kicking the door until he heard footsteps coming towards him. "About time! I told you…" Malik looked confused as he walked in the suite. The door was answered by a female who looked just as confused as he was. He looked around and realized he was in the wrong room.

"Are you crazy knocking on my door like that? I was up all night studying and I wake up to some fool banging on my door. May I help you?"

"I'm sorry. I thought I thought this was my room."

"Well it's not! The door says 435 and the last I checked, the fourth floor was all females so could you kindly turn around and leave? I have three more hours of sleep to get before my chemistry final. Thanks bye!" The female pushed Malik back out the door and shut it in his face.

Malik took off running to the elevator and began franticly pushing the up button. He couldn't believe he'd gotten off at the wrong floor. He also couldn't believe he had never seen such a beautiful female before in his life. He thought to himself 'How is it I've been here almost a year and have never seen her?' As he completed his thought the door to the elevator opened. Malik jumped on the elevator and took it to the fifth floor becoming frantic again as he looked at his watch and realized he was now ten minutes late for class.

Malik spent the rest of his afternoon thinking about the girl from the dorms. He was glad that he had turned in his last project for the semester and had completed most of his finals. It gave him time to think of a way to get the girls name and number. He closed his eyes and imagined her standing in the room. He remembered how her hazel eyes shined and how cute she looked with her hair tied up. He had to see her again. His phone rang distracting him from his thoughts. It was his mother. He had just remembered it was her birthday before he answered the phone. "*Happy Birthday to you, Happy Birthday to you, Happy Birthday dear Mamaaaaaa, Happy Birthday tooooo yoooooooooou!* Hey mom! How's your birthday going so far?"

"Boy please stop trying to serenade me like I'm one of them dumb chicken-heads from your school!" Kim yelled while she chuckled. "But thank you for remembering. How was your finals?"

"My finals start in a week. I had some projects to turn in before then that I just finished. I think I did pretty good." Malik had a little disdain in his tone. The one thing that annoyed him about his mother was the way she talked. She had a terrible tendency of not using proper grammar and annunciation and it was only when she spoke to people she was close with. It was as if they didn't deserve to hear proper grammar.

"Well, whas wrong witchu?"

"Nothing, I'm ok. I just miss you." He hated lying but he knew telling her the truth would only offend her.

"Awe I miss you too boy. Did you start packing? I put the reservation in to fly down there to help you drive the U-Haul back. You know you have to put those reservations in early or you'll get stuck with one of those trailer thingys. I don't know who they think got a truck to be hooking that thing on to."

"Mom, I forgot to tell you I'm taking summer classes so I won't be coming home. I've got a job now and I was thinking about saving up money over the summer to put down on an apartment."

"Malik! Why didn't you tell me? I don't know why you trying to work anyway. All that money your daddy done gave me for you. You should just use it to pay for the apartment, a class, a book or something."

"I don't want his damn money mama!"

"Hey you betta watch ya tone! I'll fly down there quicker than you can blink and knock you in ya head! Respect what your daddy did! He could've acted like you didn't exist. Malik, I've explained this to you over and over again. He didn't find out I was pregnant until I went into labor."

"But he found out he was married before he met you right?"

"Malik that's not the point. He did the stand up thing in sending me money to take care of you."

"The stand up thing would've been to actually be there for me. Ma I don't want to do this right now. I want to talk about your birthday. What are your plans?"

"Well I was hoping to take you to meet your daddy since we're on the subject."

"We're not on the subject and I don't want to meet him." Malik said sarcastically. He rolled his eyes and shook his head. He wished his mother understood how difficult it was for him to know he was the result of an affair.

Kim paused before she responded. She took a deep breathe and sighed in Malik's ear. "Malik, it's good to know where you come from. It helps you understand who you are. It gives you validation."

"I don't want and need his validation. Ma I really don't want to talk about this right now or ever for that matter. Look I have to go charge my phone."

"Malik don't hang up. I'm sorry for pressuring you. I just; never mind. Listen baby, I'm ok with you taking the summer classes but we need to talk about this apartment thing. You have a scholarship and I don't want you messing up your grades because you have to work to pay rent. I really want you to think about using that money for your apartment at least."

"I'll think about it, I promise."

"Thank you. Well, I'm about to go to the spa. Greg is treating me to a full body massage and a facial. He's so fancy!"

"Alright, well have fun ma and I'll check in with you tomorrow. I love you"

"Love you too baby!"

Malik thought about mailing his mother a card telling her how much he appreciates her. He had already sent her three cards for her birthday but he wanted to send a special just because card. As he was thinking about it, an idea flashed in his head and he immediately put his plan in action.

Malik got nervous as he walked up to room 435. He began to tip toe as he got closer to the door. He bent down to try to see if he could hear anyone in the room when he felt the pressure of a knee in the middle of this back. Malik was so startled that he almost peed himself.

"What are you doing at my door?"

Malik counted to five and ducked his head while he turned and grabbed the leg. The person fell on their back and began kicking Malik with her other leg. He grabbed her other legged and laughed as she tried to squirm out of his grip.

"Let me go you jerk! Why are you stalking me? Just wait until I get loose. I'm going to kick your…"

"Calm down woman! I was coming to apologize to you and this is how I get treated?"

"Well it looked like you were being a peeping Tom if you ask me! Let my legs go!"

"I'll let them go when you calm down!"

"You've got five seconds to let my legs go or I'll scream at the top of my lungs. I promise you'll get locked up!"

"Fine have it your way!" Malik tossed her legs to the ground and ran down the hall. She got up to follow him but didn't move fast enough and lost him on the stairs. She walked back to her room upset and a little paranoid believing she had a stalker. When she opened her door, she noticed an envelope on the floor in the doorway. She picked it up and opened it. On the front of the card was a picture of a little girl with her hand on her mouth and the word 'Oops' underneath of it. She opened the card and began to read the handwritten note on the inside.

'I know I startled you this morning when I banged on your door. Even though it wasn't on purpose I still want to apologize to you for disturbing you. I think it was fate that had me go to the wrong floor because other wise I would have never met you. I would like to take you out if you'll allow me to. I'm in dorm room 535 so if you think I'm worth spending your time with please meet me in the fifth floor lobby at 7 pm. If not, I'll understand and I won't bother you anymore. By the way, I hope you did well on your Chemistry exam.

Hope to see you tonight,
Malik'

Gabrielle placed the card back in the envelope and smirked while she shook her head. She said out loud to herself,

"He wasn't a stalker after all. Poor fool probably left this in the door right before I walked up." Gabrielle sighed and placed the card on her desk as she walked over to lie down on her bed. She contemplated if she would actually meet him and got really nervous. Then she felt bad about the whole altercation that just happened. She realized he wasn't peeping to be a voyeur but to see if she was in her room to get the card. Gabrielle got the bright idea to leave him a card apologizing for the events that had just occurred. She found some construction paper in her top drawer of her dresser and began to put her artistic abilities to good use.

Malik looked at the clock on his desk for the eighteenth time and it still wasn't seven o'clock. He got nervous thinking she wouldn't show and felt stupid for embarrassing her twice in one day. He realized he didn't know her name and felt even more stupid for running off afterwards. 'She must really think I'm a stalker! Oh I know she's not going to show.' Malik shook the thoughts out of his head and tried his best to be optimistic. He looked at the clock and saw that it was six forty five. He grabbed his jacket and walked down the hall to the lobby area near the fifth floor elevator. He jumped out of the love seat every time he heard the bell for the elevator ring. He had been sitting there for five minutes and gave up hope. "She's not coming. I'm so stupid. I don't even know if she got the card. I don't even know her name. What was I thinking?"

Malik got up off the love seat and shook his head. He began to walk toward his dorm room and noticed a card taped to the door. He looked around to see who had left it. His name was written in a fancy script on the front of the envelope. He opened it up to see a sketch of a butterfly. When he looked closer at the butterfly he realized that it was made out of words that read:

I read your letter and I appreciate it. Don't think you're off the hook from banging on my door or peeping in my door. You know what? Maybe you just like my door? Malik, I think you're very sweet for doing what you did but unfortunately I can't meet you for dinner at seven because I already have plans for tonight. So here's a ticket to the theatre on campus. Take yourself out and enjoy. Maybe we can get together at a later time. Thanks for the offer though.

Gabrielle.'

Malik felt a little relieved after reading the letter and was a little disappointed that he couldn't meet up with her. On the other hand, he was excited that he finally knew her name, Gabrielle. Malik took the ticket for the theatre and placed it in his pants pocket. He decided to go to the theatre since Gabrielle had probably spent money on the ticket. As he changed his clothes he began thinking of ways to get close to Gabrielle. There was something about her that drew Malik to her.

As Malik walked into the theatre he heard the most beautiful female voice. He quietly snuck into the back of the theatre as to not make any noise. He didn't want to disrupt the songstress. As he sat down, he looked at the stage and noticed a familiar beautiful face that went with the voice he heard. It was Gabrielle. She was singing 'Everything I Do' by Brandy. He closed his eyes and took in the sound of Gabrielle's voice and hoped she wouldn't stop singing. Malik shook his head and sighed. He couldn't believe he was feeling this way about someone he didn't really know. Malik watched the rest of the play in awe. He never knew how exciting the theatre could be.

Chapter Sixteen

Two weeks had gone by and Malik had not heard from Gabrielle. It was as if she never existed. He went to her dorm room and left several notes for her. It was the end of the semester and once summer came, he would have to rely on fate to have them cross each others paths. "I don't even know her last name to look her up in the directory. This is crazy! Why am I sitting here talking about a girl to myself?" Malik sighed and decided to call it a night. He had his last final at seven in the morning and didn't want to be late. Just as he was dozing off he heard a light knock at his door. He jumped up and turned his table lamp on.

"Who is it?"

"My name's Cherise. You don't know me but we have a mutual friend, Gabrielle."

Malik ran and grabbed the door. He let Cherise in and turned the wall light on as she walked in.

"Gabrielle asked me to give this to you. She's out of intensive care but she's still not doing too well. She wanted to..."

"Intensive care? What are you talking about? I just saw her two weeks ago at the play and she was fine."

"Oh my gosh! You don't know? I'm sorry, I thought you knew."

"Knew what? What happened?"

"Gabrielle was in a car accident. She went out with a couple of friends after the play and a drunk driver hit her car. She was in a coma for a few days. She had some hemorrhaging and they're having trouble controlling the bleeding. Her head went through the windshield. Like I said she's doing better now but she still has a while to go before she'll be able to walk."

"What! Where is she?"

"She's at County Hospital."

Malik looked up at the ceiling to control his tears. He couldn't believe he was tearing up over this.

"I'm sorry, I thought her god mother would've told you. Gabrielle keeps talking about how you guys met." Cherise lightly chuckled. "I think it was so cute of you to send that letter."

"I need to see her." Malik said in a serious tone.

Cherise straightened her face when she realized how upset Malik was. "Visiting hours are over for the day but they start at ten tomorrow. She's in room 535. Funny, that's your dorm room number. Guess it won't be hard for you to remember. Well, I have to go but here's the card she wanted me to give you."

"Thank you. Thank you very much."

"Good night Malik.

"Good night."

Gabrielle had just gotten back from getting testing done when she saw Malik standing in the doorway of her hospital room. "Hi. I didn't expect to see you here."

"Who's this sweetie?" Gabrielle's godmother asked as she walked out of the bathroom.

"This is Malik. The guy I was telling you about. You know the one I thought was a stalker."

"Oh yes, good to meet you Malik, I hope."

"Hello ma'am."

"Malik, this is my godmother Elizabeth Holden."

"Please call me Miss Liz honey. I'm only Elizabeth when I'm handling business affairs."

"Yes ma'am."

"Yes ma'am? Sweetie please relax! You would've thought someone died in here!"

"Yes ma'am I mean Miss Liz"

Liz smirked as she walked closer to Malik. "You know you have a very familiar face sweetheart. Who's your daddy?"

"My mother raised me. I don't know much about my father. I look like my mom though." Malik said.

"God mom, stop! You're embarrassing me!" Gabrielle yelled!

'Well, I'm going to get some air. I'll leave you two to talk until the doctor comes back with those results. Are you alright Gabby?" Liz smirked at Gabrielle as she walked out the door.

"Yes I'm ok for now. Thanks."

"Well I'll be a holler away if you need me. And by the way, he does look like a model."

Gabrielle blushed from cheek to cheek and put her head down. Malik laughed as he walked over to her bedside.

"So how are you? I got your letter. Your friend Cherise came by my room last night and told me what happened."

"I'm doing ok I guess. I have this terrible pain in my head. They put like twenty stitches in my head. The doctor said I was lucky I didn't go all the way through the windshield."

"Wow. I uh I thought you had forgotten about me. Not that you were suppose to remember me or anything like that. It's just that, never mind, it's not important now. So how long are you going to be in here?"

"Well, they ran some more tests because I was hemorrhaging for a while and I had a lot of blood loss. I'm not sure when I'll be leaving. I'm upset I'm going to miss my finals. My god mother talked to my teachers though so I'll take them once I'm out of here."

"What about your parents? If you don't mind me asking, how come they aren't here?"

"No, its cool. My mom died of cancer when I was six and my godmother was helping my father raise me until I was sixteen. He died in an accident at work. My godmother's been raising me since then."

"Oh wow, sorry to hear that. Like I said earlier, I don't really know my father. My mom got married when I was ten but my stepdad's been there for me since I was seven."

Gabrielle looked as if she was fighting to keep her eyes open and her light toned skin began to look pale. Malik stood beside her and placed his hand on hers and noticed it felt cold. "Gabrielle, are you ok?" Malik shook her arm and her head leaned to her right shoulder. Alarms started going off on the monitors to the right of Gabrielle's bed. Malik ran out the room to grab a nurse. As he passed the bed, he noticed the middle of the sheet on top of Gabrielle was covered in blood.

"Nurse! Nurse! Somebody help. She's bleeding!"

Gabrielle's doctor followed by Liz rushed passed Malik into Gabrielle's room. Malik stood outside the hospital room looking through the window as the doctor and nurses worked on Gabrielle. He heard her monitors beeping and got nervous. Malik paced the hall for a few minutes and couldn't take the nervousness any more. He left the hospital and went back to his room to clear his head.

"God, I don't normally pray to you very often but when I do you know it's normally for other people. Please don't let Gabrielle die Lord. She doesn't deserve this. I mean she's already lost both of her parents and it just wouldn't seem fair for her to not live the life they may have wanted her to live. On top of that, I feel like I know her and I want an opportunity to get to know her better. So, I'm just asking you to help her get better so that she can live a happy healthy normal life. Even if that means I'll never get to see her again. I love you Lord and I promise I'll spend more time praying and reading my Bible. Thank you. Amen."

Malik got up off his knees from the side of his bed and sighed very deeply. His mode was disturbed by the ringing of his phone.

"Hello."

"Is this Malik?"

"Yes, who's this?" Malik asked confusingly.

"This is Mrs. Liz, Gabrielle's god mother."

"Oh I'm sorry, I didn't recognize your voice. How is she?"

"She's stable for now. She lost a lot of blood. She needs a liver transplant. I know this sounds strange but would you mind coming down and getting tested? I've been calling all of her friends in hopes of finding a match. Since both her parents are gone and I don't have contact info for a lot of her family, this is going to be a difficult challenge. The thing is, the sooner they can find a match, the better."

"A liver transplant?" Malik's voice faded as he said the words. He had a fear of having any type of surgery. He even hated getting physicals. The thought of him having to be cut open made him queasy.

"Malik. Are you there?"

"Yes ma'am. Sorry, this is just a lot to take in. Umm I need to think. I have to call my mom."

"I don't mean to lay this on you. From talking to Gabrielle and her room mate, you guys haven't known each other that long so I can see how awkward this is for me to ask. Listen Malik, can you at least get tested to see if you're a match? We can talk about the surgery after the results come back if you are indeed a match."

"Can I call you back? I really need to talk to my mom first."

"Yes, yes I understand sweet heart."

"I promise I'll contact you once I talk to her."

"Sure. And Malik, thank you for even considering doing this. It really means a lot to both Gabrielle and I."

"I understand. I'll be in touch. Good bye."

"Good bye."

Malik could sense the tension and urgency in Mrs. Liz's voice. He could also tell that she had been crying. He thought about Gabrielle's mom and how Gabrielle was the only connection Mrs. Liz had left to her friend. Malik sighed again. "I sure have been sighing a lot lately. Lord, what am I going to do?"

Chapter Seventeen

(Two Weeks Later)

Malik picked up his phone in his dorm room and dialed his mom's number. He hesitated before he hit the send button on his phone and hoped she wouldn't answer.

"Hey baby! How are you?" Kim said in a cheerful voice.

Malik hesitated before he responded. "I'm good Ma. How's everything going up there?"

"What's up Malik?" Kim's voice had quickly changed to a serious tone. She could hear the nervousness in Malik's voice.

"Ma, I'm just checking on you. You know I miss you a lot and wish you would come down here to see me since I won't be home this summer."

"So you're a match huh?"

"Huh? What? Ma, I'm just calling to say hey."

"Malik, how old are you?"

"Ma."

"How old are you Malik?"

"I'm nineteen."

"And as a nineteen year old, do you think your mama that's 41 and has always known when you were lying, when you were scared, when you were hungry, when you just needed a hug wouldn't know when something is off with you?"

"Yes Ma."

"So, answer my question!"

"Yes, I'm a match. How did you know I went through with the test anyway?"

"Malik, for a college student, you're not the smartest in the bunch. You put the house number down as the contact number. They called earlier today to let you know the results were in."

"Oh. Ma, listen, I know you said I'd be a fool to help someone out that I don't really know and that I shouldn't get involved but I couldn't help it. I've spent as much time as I could over the past three weeks with Gabrielle and she's amazing. She's funny and smart and she gets me. It's like we're twins or something. I'd swear if her parents weren't dead that we were related. You have to understand…"

"I have to understand that you're my son, my son and I don't want anything to happen to you. Malik, you're talking about surgery on an organ in your body. Do you know what that means? I don't want to loose you just so you can play Mr. Macho and save the damsel in distress!"

"I talked to the doctor Ma, and I'm her only hope. She would have to wait years to find a match and who knows if she'll live that long. What if this was the reason why our paths crossed. So I can help her. There has to be a reason for all this happening. I've been praying Ma and I think God will keep me safe through the surgery and we'll both come out okay. The surgeon has done plenty of procedures and has never lost a patient. You know how I feel about surgery so I'm not taking this lightly. I need to know you'll support me Ma. Tell me you'll be there for me. I need you Ma, I need you."

"So you're intending on doing this no matter what I say?"

"I would hope you would be there for me but yes I will."

"Fine, just know I'm not happy about this at all!"

"Thank you Ma, I love you."

"I love you too boy. So when is all this happening?"

"They're scheduling to do the procedure next Thursday morning at ten. Can you make it down here? Gabrielle's god mom is letting me stay at their house until I recover. She's going to pay for a nurse for me and everything. I found an apartment but I don't move in until July fifteenth."

"Next Thursday? Malik, I'll see if I can get off to come down Tuesday. We can stay in a hotel. We don't have to stay at that women's house. We don't even know her like that. How long will it take for you to recover anyway?"

"The doctor said I should be one hundred percent within two weeks. Listen Ma, Gabrielle is all that Mrs. Liz has left. She's just really happy that I've agreed to do this. She wants to make everything as easy as possible."

"So, she already knows you're a match? Well I see where I fall on the totem pole!"

"Ma, it wasn't like that, the hospital called her earlier and told her."

"It would've been easier if you weren't a match! I need to talk to this Mrs. Liz before any thing goes down. What's her number?"

"I already told her you would want to talk to her. She's going to call you tonight. I hope you don't mind I gave her the house number."

"Well, you already gave it to the hospital so why not just give it to the rest of the world!"

"Sorry Ma. Thanks again. You and Greg can fly down Tuesday morning. I know he won't let you be gone without him for too long. Oh yeah, and don't worry about the plane tickets. Mrs. Liz has got you covered."

"You know that's right! Greg would be calling every ten minutes the entire time I was gone. Malik, we can fly down ourselves. We don't need her to do that. I'll just call the airline and book the flight."

Malik smirked, "Ma, she has her own jet. You and Greg can leave whatever time you want to."

"Well excuse the heck out of me! Okay, well I can't wait to hear from Mrs. Liz. Baby, I gotta go. I have a meeting in fifteen minutes and I want to put the request in for time off as soon as possible. I love you Malik."

"Love you too Ma. Bye"

"Bye."

Chapter Eighteen

Malik stood on the platform with Liz near the landing pad where the private plane was landing. He was excited to see his mother. It had been six months and he missed her everyday he was in school. Liz grabbed Malik's arm to keep him from going toward the landing pad. Malik looked back at Liz with an attitude on his face.

"It's not safe yet. You have to wait for the propeller's to stop."

Malik nodded his head in submission and waited for his mother and step-father to get off the pane. He began to bite his nails as the impatience built up. He heard the engine go off and the cabin door of the plane opened. Liz let go of his arm and Malik ran over to the steps of the plane.

"Ma!"

"Hey baby! Why are you so hype? You act like you haven't seen me in years."

"It's felt like years! Did you bring me some of those homemade cookies I like?"

"And how are you?"

"I'm sorry Ma, how are you? Do you need help with anything? Did you bring those homemade cookies I like?"

Liz walked up beside Malik and put her right hand on his left shoulder. "The help will take care of the luggage. Hello, I'm Elizabeth Holden but you can call me Liz."

"Hello, I'm Kim and this is my husband Greg.'

"Its nice to finally meet you in person Kim. Greg, it's good to meet you too."

Kim and Greg both shook Liz's hand and followed her and Malik into the house.

"This is the estate," Liz said. "My late husband's family lived here many years ago. They left the house to him when they passed away. Unfortunately my husband past away a few years ago and everything was left to me. Like I told you on the phone Kim, I am very fortunate to have everything that I do but I wasn't always as well off as I am now. I'm just grateful to God for blessing me the way He did."

"I'm sorry about your husband Liz," Kim said.

"Thank you," said Liz.

"This is a beautiful home. So it's just you and Gabrielle?"

"Yes. Just the two of us."

Liz grinned at Malik and turned to Kim. "I don't know how I would've made it through that tough time if I didn't have Gabrielle. She reminds me so much of her mother. She's what has kept me going. So I hope you see now, why I've been fighting so hard to keep her with me."

"I understand a whole lot better now Liz," Kim replied.

The butler walked past everyone in the foyer and carried the luggage up the stairs. As he passed, they all began to follow Liz to the family room.

"So, can we go over the details for the procedure if you don't mind Liz? This whole situation is happening so fast and I want to be sure every I is dotted and every T is crossed" said Kim.

"I agree one hundred percent," replied Liz as she walked over and picked up a manila folder that sat on top of a white marble mantle over top of the fire place. Malik, Kim and Greg sat down on the love seats that faced each other. "We meet with Dr. Schowe tomorrow morning at ten am. He's the surgeon that will be performing the surgery. They're going to make sure Malik doesn't have any type of infection. Then they will prep him for surgery and explain the procedure and how it will affect him. We have to be at the surgery center in the hospital by 5 am Thursday morning. We'll be able to see the surgery from the observation room. Oh and I almost forgot Malik, you cannot eat or drink anything at least twelve hours before surgery."

"Ok. Well, Malik, you better get to bed baby. You have a long couple of days ahead." Kim said as she tapped Malik on his leg.

"Ma, I'm not ten anymore. It's only eight. I'm going to take a swim in the pool, if that's ok with you Mrs. Liz."

"I think that's up to your mother honey. You may be nineteen but if memory serves me correct, you're not grown yet. And your mother's right, your body is going to undergo a lot of stress over the next couple of days. You might want to take it easy."

"I'm almost a grown man. I can hang."

"Malik, your mother said bed so bed it is. This is not the time to be fighting her on this." Greg said in a stern voice.

"Yes sir. What time should I be ready by in the morning?"

"The car will pick us up around eighty thirty."

"Well, good night everyone."

"Good night Malik. I'll be up to talk to you in a minute." Kim said.

Malik somberly walked up the stairs feeling a little defeated. He hated being embarrassed in front of Mrs. Liz like he was a child. He also knew better than to back talk to Greg. He may not be his father but he's been there for him the majority of his life and that made Malik respect him even the more. He could hear his parents and Mrs. Liz talking as he walked up the stairs.

"Kim I know you and Greg have your reservations about the surgery. The doctor reassured me that Malik will be completely ok. His liver should begin to regenerate itself almost immediately."

"Listen Liz, my wife and I have discussed this extensively and even with out apprehensions we do understand how rare of a situation this is. We don't think that Malik and Gabrielle connected with each other when they did by mistake. I know that the Lord works in mysterious ways and this just may be one of those ways."

"Malik has always been a special and unique child. When he gets determined about helping someone, we've learned to just step back and let him. As long as he's not in harms way we don't question it. That doesn't mean we don't inquire. We just don't want to stop him from things he's passionate about and he appears to be very passionate about your goddaughter."

"Gabrielle and I both are very grateful to you for allowing Malik to donate apart of his liver. I want to take you to meet Gabrielle tomorrow after the doctor visit. I'm sure she wants to thank you in person."

"Yes, we would like that." Kim said as she held Greg's hand. "I did want to know though, where are Gabrielle's parents? Why haven't we heard anything from them?"

"Gabrielle's mother died when she was around six. Her stepfather raised her up until a few years ago when he died from an accident on his construction site. I was helping Hernando raise

Gabrielle and he left custody of her to me when he passed. Hernando never got to tell Gabrielle that he wasn't her birth father and I just haven't had the heart to tell her myself. Her mother had her under unusual circumstances and lets just say her father really didn't want to have anything to do with her."

"I understand that completely. Malik's father and I were not officially together when I got pregnant with him so naturally he wasn't there for Malik. Fortunately he has helped take care of him financially."

"I can say the same for Gabrielle's father. Being that I'm pretty well off, I've decided to just keep the money in a trust for Gabrielle until she's twenty five. She has a full scholarship for college so she won't really need the money until then."

"Honey, I think we should unpack our stuff before we hit the hay." Greg said as he rubbed Kim's thigh.

"Greg's right, we all have a long rest of the week and rest is essential. I won't be here when you get up in the morning. I'm going to spend some time with Gabrielle before we go to see Dr. Schowe. The cook is usually here by six am though so just let him know what you'd like and he'll whip it right on up for you. Malik has taken advantage of Javier's cooking already."

"I'm sure of it," said Kim.

"Let me show you to your suite."

"Oh yes, our suite." Kim said with a sarcastic undertone. Could you also show me where Malik's room is?"

"Sure, it's right next to yours.

"Ok. Thanks."

Kim knocked on Malik's door and peeped her head in. He was laying on the bed watching television. "Hey, can I talk to you for a minute Malik?"

"Yeah Ma, what's up?"

"I just want you to know I'm very proud of you. You've decided to do a very brave thing and even though I'm very nervous about the whole surgery part, you've made the right choice. Just make sure you heal quickly or I'm gonna have to open up a can of whip…"

"Ma!"

"Huh? Oh, sorry baby, I zoned out for a second. I can't let anything happen to you. The day I had you changed my life. You don't know how I used to be and I would never want you to find out. Just know that you bring out the best in me and I'm grateful to God for it."

"Ma, I'm going to be ok. I promise!"

"You better be!" Kim said fighting back tears. She didn't want Malik to know how nervous she was about the whole situation. Kim walked over and hugged Malik for a while until Greg walked into the room and put his arm on Kim's shoulder.

"He's going to be okay Babe. Lets go to bed." Greg gently placed his arms around Kim's waist until she let go of Malik. Greg patted Malik on the shoulder and placed his arm around Kim's waist as they walked out the room. Malik watched them and thought about how blessed he was to have two parent's that really cared about him.

As Malik cut off the television he began to pray for his family and for Gabrielle's family. He wanted God to show him why he was so connected to someone he had just met a few months ago. He asked God to keep him safe through the surgery and also asked God to heal Gabrielle quickly. Malik turned his light off and fell right to sleep.

Chapter Nineteen

It had been two weeks since Malik had donated a part of his liver to Gabrielle. Gabrielle had recovered very well and was due to be released from the hospital that afternoon. Malik got excited every time he heard foot steps come up the marble steps. He sat up in his bed and tried to peek his head to the left far enough to be able to see out the window. He had been given strict orders by his mother to stay in the bed and even though she had returned to Maryland two days prior, he still felt like his mother was there with him. Malik grew tired waiting to hear Mrs. Liz and Gabrielle come home and decided to go to sleep.

"Malik! Oh Malik! I have a surprise for you." Liz sang up the stairs to Malik.

Malik jumped up out of bed and could feel the soreness in his stomach. He still had to wait for the muscles in his stomach to grow back together. Malik took his time getting to the door and peeked out down the hall to see his mother standing there with her arms opened wide.

"I thought I told you not to get out of bed!"

"Ma, what are you doing here? I thought you wouldn't be back until next week."

"Yeah, well they approved me for family leave so I have some more time to spend with my baby."

"That's what's up mom. I'm glad you're back. Mrs. Liz, is Gabrielle still coming home today?"

Liz walked up the stairs and stood next to Kim. She looked over Malik's shoulder and smiled. Malik turned around to see Gabrielle sitting in a wheel chair behind them.

"I've been home for a few hours now but you sleep so heavy a hurricane could've came through here and you wouldn't know it!"

Malik slowly made his way toward Gabrielle. Kim rushed up beside him to help him walk. "Take your time baby. She's gonna be here for a while."

Gabrielle attempted to stand up to hug Malik and fell back in her chair. Liz ran to her side to help her get back in the wheel chair comfortably. "Gabby honey, recovery takes time. You've lost a lot of blood and just had major surgery in the matter of a month. Take it easy."

"I will. I will. Can't help but wanting to be superwoman."

"Right, that's what it is, superwoman." Malik said as he laughed at Gabrielle.

"Ha ha ha Malik. You thought I was superwoman enough to ask me out."

"And look how that turned out. I'm sorry, I didn't mean it like that."

"It's ok, you're still a jerk and I'm still superwoman." Gabrielle said as she smirked at Malik.

"I think it's time for both of you to get something to eat. I'll have Javier start dinner." Liz said as she pushed Gabrielle to the elevator. "What would you like Malik?"

"Whatever Gabrielle wants. It's her first day back in civilization."

"Well, Gabrielle will be eating applesauce and tomato soup."

"Ok, in that case, I'll have grilled cheese and tomato soup. I'm not a fan of applesauce and that won't do anything to my appetite."

"Then it's settled." Liz said as she stood behind Gabrielle to push her wheel chair to the elevator. Malik would you like to ride down on the elevator or are you brave enough to take the stairs?"

"I'll take the stairs." Malik said in a voice much deeper than his normal voice.

Gabrielle chuckled in her wheel chair and softly mimicked Malik's voice causing Liz and Kim to laugh as well.

Malik shook his head and smirked as he walked toward the staircase. Kim walked beside Malik and helped him down the staircase one step at a time. She walked him over to the dining room table and pulled the chair out for him to sit down.

After dinner, Malik and Gabrielle sat in the family room and watched television while Kim and Liz had coffee in the sitting room.

"You know this house hasn't had this much company since my husband and daughter died. Gabrielle moved in a few years later and by that time, my life was a lot quieter."

"I can imagine. How have you been holding up through everything? I mean you've lost your husband and daughter, not to mention your best friend and then this scare with Gabrielle; that must've paid a toll on your nerves."

Liz shook her head as tears swell up in her eyes. "I've done the best I could to stay strong for Gabby. She needs me to be strong. I've just been praying and asking God for strength and that He have mercy on Gabrielle. She's so young and has a long life ahead of her. I just want to see her enjoy that life and I'll do whatever it takes to make it possible. I had no control over what happened to my husband and daughter and even Lydia, Gabrielle's mother, but I had a choice when it came to Gabrielle and as you can see, I stop at nothing for the people I love."

"Trust me I know what you mean. Malik is my heart. Having him allowed me to see how a bad situation can bring some good into your life. I had him under very strange circumstances and unfortunately because of that his father's never been in his life."

"I thought Greg was Malik's father." Liz said in a confused voice.

"Oh no, I met Greg when Malik was a little boy. We got married fifteen years ago. He's the father Malik knows. His real father was unbeknownst to me married to someone else when Malik was conceived. It was such a shocker to me. I found out at a church revival he was preaching at. A few weeks later I took a home pregnancy test. It was positive and I was completely devastated. I had just about made my mind up that I wasn't going to keep the baby and then I saw the ultrasound photo and it melted my hard heart. I had planned on not telling Malik's father at all mainly because I didn't have a way to get in contact with him. I just so happened to hear that he was in town doing another crusade and I went up to his hotel room and banged on the door until someone opened it. I was nine months pregnant by then and ended up telling him I was pregnant and delivering the baby on the hotel couch in the same night."

"Are you serious?"

"Yes, I tell you I was standing in the doorway talking to his assistant; I think her name was Stacy or something like that. All I know is my water broke and next thing I knew, my legs were propped up on the couch and I was pushing."

"Wow. Does Malik know this story?"

"Nah, he doesn't like to hear about stuff like that. He is just fine with knowing as little about his father as possible. Malik's father has been sending me money since he was an infant and Malik won't even touch that."

"Gabrielle doesn't know about her birth father. Her mother got married to Hernando a few months after Gabrielle was born. Her birth father has been sending her money since she was two years old but by her mother's request; I put the money in a trust for Gabrielle to have access to when she is twenty one. Her mother also asked that I wait until that time to tell Gabrielle the truth. She wrote her a letter to read on her twenty first birthday that will explain everything to her."

Kim shook her head and sighed, "It's amazing how you can live life and pretend that someone doesn't exist and think giving them money is going to replace you not being in their life."

Liz immediately became convicted and began to think about Cyndi. She hadn't talked to her since she found out she was the one that killed her daughter. Liz had been checking on her periodically and knew she had just gone back into rehab. She covered the bill for her stay at the rehab center and requested that Cyndi not know she was paying for everything. Liz made up in her mind that she was going to plan and see Cyndi soon.

Liz came out of her trance and turned back to Kim. "I think it's time we get the kids to bed!"

"Right, I'm sure they won't sleep but at least they'll be settled in their rooms."

Chapter Twenty

Three weeks had gone by since Gabrielle had been out of the hospital. Liz had gotten her settled in and she was having a physical therapist come a few hours a day three times a week to help her regain strength in her legs and arms. Gabrielle was almost completely back to her old self and she and Malik had grown quite close. Liz had let Malik use the garage as a work station to practice his woodworking. He was selling items and saving the money up to place a deposit on his apartment. Liz had connected Malik with a few wealthy friends of hers that were fond of his work. By the end of July, Malik had at least three orders per week.

"Malik, your mothers on the phone." Gabrielle said through the intercom in her room.

"Ok, I got it." He said as he spoke into the intercom in the garage.

"Hey Ma. How's it going?"

"Hey honey, I'm good. How's everything going with the apartment? Are you ready to move in yet?"

"Yeah, you wouldn't believe how much money I've made over the past month. My work is selling like crazy."

"I'm proud of you honey! How's the roommate situation going? Is Craig moving with you?"

"No, his mom wants him to stay on campus and since she's paying for him to go to school he has no say."

"Awe, I'm sorry honey. Well you know you do have some money stored up. Just say the word and I'll put it in your account. You could pay for the whole year up front."

"Ma, I don't wanna touch that money. I'll be fine. I put a poster up on campus. If worse comes to worse, I'll just be my own roommate!"

"Now you know I'm not comfortable with you living by yourself. Have you tried putting something in the school newsletter?"

"No. I don't want any weirdo's thinking I want a male companion. I'm not sure what I would do if some dude tried to get in the shower with me!" Malik started chuckling on the phone and Kim followed.

"You have a few weeks until the semester starts to figure things out. If you can't find a roommate then back on campus you stay. I'm serious Malik. You know we don't have any family down there and I'm just not too comfortable with you being completely by yourself. I know you'll be twenty in a few weeks but you're still my baby. Besides since you're so determined not to use the money your father's been sending for you, you would have to work extra hard to make sure you can pay rent and all the bills. You cannot afford to loose your scholarship because you're so stubborn and I won't let you!"

"How about this, you and Greg pack up your stuff and move in with me. You know you can find a job anywhere doing anything. That way you won't have to worry about me and Greg won't have to worry about you!"

"Malik please, Greg is not moving to Georgia and don't think I haven't asked him about it. I just get this feeling that you're not coming back and I'm trying to hold on to you as long as I can."

Malik could hear his mother's voice trembling in the phone. "Ma, I'll always be your baby, especially when I'm a grown man. I will admit I do like it down here and if business keeps going the way it is I may just open up a wood shop down here. Nothings definite yet though but I always know how to get back home so don't cry Ma."

"I'm not crying boy, it's my allergies." Kim said lying.

"Ok, well I hope your allergies get better soon." Malik said with a smirk on his face.

"Honey, Greg is summoning me. We're on our way to the flower store to pick up some things for the garden. The season will be changing soon and we need to prepare the ground."

"Ok Ma. I love you and I'll be up for my birthday so I'll see you in September."

"Before you go honey, I wasn't going to mention it but I contacted your father while you were in the hospital. He lives right near campus. I know you don't want to have anything to do with him but just remember that he's only one part of another whole family that you have. You do have older brothers and sisters that you should meet. I think its time since you're becoming a man and all."

"I'll think about it. Good bye Ma."

"Malik?"

He could hear the desperation in his mother's voice. " Yes Ma."

"I love you."

"Love you too Ma. Tell Greg I said 'Hi" and I'll be home in September"

"I will. Good bye."

"Good bye."

Malik sat the phone down on the charger and paced his floor. He could not understand why it was so important to his mother that he get to know his father and his family. Every time he even thought about his father he became enraged and he had never met him. All he knew was that he hurt his mother and that was all he needed to know. He had his father's number this whole time and never realized that it was a Georgia number. There was a reason for that; he didn't care enough to connect the two. He plopped down on the work chair in the garage and started scratching his head. Maybe it was time his father saw the man he was becoming and how he had nothing to do with it. Malik was startled by Gabrielle walking up behind him and putting her hand on his shoulder.

"I'm sorry, I was calling you on the intercom but you didn't answer. I thought you might have chopped off a finger or something."

"Oh, no I'm fine. I was just thinking."

"Well it must've been some really deep thinking to not hear me yelling your name."

Malik shook his head, "Trust me, it was pretty deep."

"Well, what's up? You know I'm a psych major, I need all the training I can get."

Malik looked at Gabrielle and realized how much he was falling for her and she probably had no idea. He gave her a half smile and pulled up a stool for her to sit on.

Gabrielle sat down and turned towards Malik, she put her left hand on his left knee and looked him in the eyes, "Now how can I help you?"

Malik immediately got hard and scooted back a little on his stool. He kept telling himself in his head that his mama raised a gentleman and that's what he's going to be. "My mom wants me to meet my father, my real father. She said he lives in Georgia near here and she wants me to meet his family, or my family. You know what I mean."

"Yes, I do. And how do you feel about all of this? You never really talk about your real father at all besides calling him a selfish horny bastard that you will never be like."

"Right. I don't know what I feel. I mean I'm so angry just thinking about how he left my mom and everything she went through raising me by herself. I get even more upset about the fact that he has been sending me money like that's supposed to make up for him not being there. What makes me really upset is that my mom keeps pushing me to meet him and talk to him. Like that's supposed to make me feel better or change the way I feel about him. He's still a jerk and he doesn't deserve to even see my face!"

"Calm down Malik. You have to look outside the box for a minute. Imagine if there's a whole other part to who you are that you'll never know because you want to punish your father. In reality you're actually punishing yourself. He's not angry with you or disappointed by you, he just wants to have you in his life. Isn't that what you wanted all along? That's all you keep talking about. You deserve to make him tell you why he left and you also deserve to be made whole. You're only short changing yourself by never taking the time to get to know the other half of who you are. So, stop being so selfish and prideful and talk to the damn man! See, now you're getting me upset!"

Gabrielle smiled at Malik and gave him a hug. She could feel how hard his penis had gotten and eased away from him. She caught herself staring at his crotch and quickly looked away. Malik looked at her with slight embarrassment and then reached in and kissed Gabrielle on the lips. Gabrielle began kissing him back and pulled Malik closer to her. Malik pulled his shirt over his head and threw it on the workstation behind them. Gabrielle started to feel a slight pain in her stomach and pushed Malik off of her as she cringed. "I'm sorry. I've been getting this sharp pain every now and then in my stomach. The doctor said it's my abdomen muscles tightening or something. Nothing serious."

Malik walked over to Gabrielle and stood behind her. He put his arms around her waist and began to rub her stomach through her shirt.

"Don't think this gets you off the hook. I really think you should talk to your father. If you want I'll go with you."

"You will?"

"Yes, just let me know and I'll be there."

"Ok, you promise?"

"Yes, I promise. Now let me go before I do something I'm going to regret."

"I'd like to see that."

"Trust me, it's not what you think. Unless kicking you in the balls is what's on your mind?"

"Oh, not at all. I've got to get in the shower anyway. I smell like a girl now."

"Well it's better than what you smelled like before that!"

"Ha, good one!"

Chapter Twenty One

Malik was shaking his leg on the couch in his new apartment waiting for Gabrielle. They had decided to be roommates and let their families know when they thought it was necessary. Gabrielle moved into the dorm the week before the fall semester and moved into Malik's apartment a week later. She had taken a large amount of money out to pay up the first few months of rent and had told Liz she used it to buy her books and some clothing for school. Malik covered Gabrielle's books that semester and she worked on campus to pay him back. Malik had been doing very well selling the woodwork he had created and was able to set up an account to have their rent taken from each month without it affecting them paying the other bills.

It was now the end of September and it was still very hot out. Malik watched the wind blow through the leaves on the tree outside their living room and wondered what this day was going to bring. He had contacted his father a week before hand and planned on meeting him today. He was nervous and anxious at the same time which only frustrated him. He had been waiting for Gabrielle to come out of her room for twenty minutes and was just about to change his mind about going when she opened the door to her room.

"Ok, I'm ready!"

"About time!"

"I'm sorry. I had to make sure I looked alright."

"You act like you're meeting you're father for the first time." Malik said in a sarcastic tone.

"I said I was sorry. Look, I know you're nervous and all but relax. He's going to love you!"

"I'm not worried about him loving me, I'm worried about the conversation we're going to have."

"Well, I'll be there as your buffer so you'll be fine."

"Can we go now?"

"Yes, let me just grab my purse."

"Girls." Malik shook his head as he stood up. He walked toward the front door of their apartment hoping Gabrielle would be behind him by the time he walked down the stairs. As he reached the bottom of the stairs he yelled up to their door, "I'm getting in the car Gabrielle. Please hurry up!"

"Coming right now! Geesh."

Malik heard Gabrielle slam the door as he reached the steps outside their apartment. He stopped for a moment, turned back around, walked back inside to the steps and looked up at Gabrielle. "Did you lock the door?"

Gabrielle stopped in her tracks without speaking, turned back around to go lock the door to their apartment.

Malik walked out the front door slamming it as he walked down the pathway to the car. Gabrielle jumped as she heard the door slam. She made a mental note to herself to not crack any jokes in the car.

As Malik pulled up to the street where Malik's father lived, Malik slowed down the car to stop at the corner. Gabrielle put her left hand on top of Malik's as he grabbed the gear shift. "Everything's going to be ok. It'll be a conversation as short or as long as you'd like it to be."

Malik put the car back in drive as he let out one deep breath, hoping for the best but preparing for the worst to happen. They pulled up in the driveway a few moments later to a beautiful single home with a small cul-de-sac in the front. As they walked up to the door a woman in her forties opened it with a lovely smile on her face.

"Hi. You must be Malik."

Malik reached out his arm to shake the woman's hand but she grabbed him and gave him a hug. He was a little caught off guard but hugged the woman back. She then stood back a few steps and looked at Malik shaking her head. "You look just like your grandfather."

"How do you know my grandfather and who are you?"

"I'm sorry suga, I'm Shannon, your father's wife your stepmother."

"Ms Shannon is fine." Malik felt Gabrielle knee him in the leg. He turned around and smirked at her. "This is my friend Gabrielle."

"Hello Ma'am."

"Well hello darling. She's beautiful Malik. Come inside please." Shannon moved into the house stretching her arm towards the sitting room. Malik and Gabrielle followed Shannon in the house to the sitting room. "You can sit in here. I'm glad you still decided to come even though your father couldn't be here."

"I'm sorry, he's not here."

"Oh no, he didn't tell you? He had to run out of town on an emergency business trip. He left early this morning. He won't be back until Monday sometime."

"Ok, I didn't know that. Well, then," Malik said sarcastically as he stood up, "I guess this was a waste of time."

Gabrielle grabbed Malik's arm pulling him back down onto the love seat. "It's not a waste of time Malik. You wanted to get to know your family and that's what we're going to do."

"That's right. Your father..."

"You mean sperm donor."

Gabrielle pushed Malik's leg.

"No, that's fine honey. I can imagine how Malik feels. He in many ways is just a sperm donor to you. I can respect that but please understand that we all have our imperfections and your sperm donors are just more evident than most peoples."

Malik looked into Shannon's eyes and could only imagine the years of hurt that his sperm donor had inflicted on her.

"I'm sorry ma'am. I had just expected this day to go a lot differently."

"I can imagine but since you're here, you might as well meet everyone."

"Everyone like who?"

"Everyone like them." Shannon opened a sliding door that connected the sitting room to a large living room area. Inside this room was a bunch of people sitting around smiling, waiting for Malik to arrive.

"Wow, umm hello."

"This is your family."

Malik stood up and walked into the living room. He was greeted by an old man that looked like an older version of Malik. "I'm your grandfather Darnell Sr." He gave Malik a big hug.

"Hi sir."

"You can call me granddad when you're ready. I know this is all new to you son but we have been waiting to meet you for years."

"Yes sir."

Shannon pulled the arms of two young women that were sitting on the chair behind Malik's grandfather. "These are your older sisters Danielle and Diane. They have the same birthday as you."

Danielle and Diane waived their arms at Malik. They each gave him a hug. Danielle spoke first, "I'm the oldest, just so you know. We're both twenty five but I was born ten minutes earlier."

"Anyway," Diane said. "As you can see Danielle has a complex issue where she thinks she has to be the best at everything. She may be a few minutes older than me but I still act older than she does."

Diane smirked at her sister as she sat back down on the love seat. Danielle followed her rolling her eyes at her sister.

A tall man walked up to Malik and shook his hand. He bore a resemblance to Malik's grandfather but also favored his mother. "I'm David, the oldest." David added an extra emphasis on 'the' as he turned and looked at Danielle. "I'm twenty seven."

"Hi David, nice to meet you."

"For the record, I just want to say that I understand the whole sperm donor thing and there are no hard feelings."

"Oh, I didn't know you heard that. I was just…"

"No need to explain man."

Malik was slightly embarrassed by the way he had responded to Shannon earlier. He looked around the room and noticed a familiar face. "Craig?"

"You guys know each other?" Shannon asked.

"Yeah, Craig was my roommate last year at Clark. He would've been my roommate this year but he said his mom was… Oh, sorry."

Craig opened his eyes real wide as if to motion Malik to stop speaking.

"You're my brother? But you don't even look like everyone else. I don't see the resemblance. You told me your dad was dead. I'm confused."

"No, I'm your cousin. My dad is dead. This is my mom, your Aunt Stephanie." Craig said as he pointed to the woman that was sitting next to him on the couch. "This is your dad's sister."

"Why didn't you tell me Craig?"

"I just found out this week when my mom told me we were coming over here Saturday to meet my cousin. I was partially in shock because I didn't know Uncle Darnell had more kids and then when she told me his son's name I was mute for a while. By the time I was going to call you, it was Saturday."

Stephanie got up from the couch and hugged Malik. "Hi nephew, I'm glad I finally get to meet you. Craig's had nothing but good things to say about you."

Malik had become so consumed in the moment he had almost forgotten Gabrielle was there. He turned around and grabbed her by the hand as he introduced her to everyone.

"This is Gabrielle Santos, my new roommate and friend. We actually share a lot more than an apartment."

Malik's grandfather cleared his throat as if to stop Malik from speaking before he got too personal.

"Oh, no, I didn't mean like that." Malik chuckled as he continued. "I gave Gabrielle apart of my kidney last spring. So we share a kidney. Ironically I was the only match which was very odd in itself since I have a rare blood type. Anyway, I asked her to come with me today. I hope you all don't mind that she's here."

"It's fine honey." Stephanie said. "The more the merrier!"

Shannon put her hand on Malik's right shoulder and looked at everyone in the living room. "I made lunch so I hope you and Gabrielle can stay."

"Yes ma'am, we would love to stay." Gabrielle said as she smiled nodding her head at Malik.

"Yes we would."

Malik and Gabrielle stayed at his father's house until almost midnight talking with his grandfather, then his siblings, then his aunt and finally his father's wife. Malik learned that he had a half sister who last Shannon heard lived in North Carolina. Unfortunately, they didn't have any information on her. The only other person that had information was Shannon's former best friend Trisha. Shannon had not spoken to her in years and wouldn't even know how to ask her for that information. Over all, Malik was glad he had come but was disappointed that he didn't meet his father. He planned on going out with his siblings to the movies the next weekend. He also promised that he would keep in contact with everyone.

Chapter Twenty Two

Malik and Gabrielle had been living together for almost three years. Liz and Kim were not too thrilled about it at first; especially since they had surprised them both by having Christmas dinner at their apartment as their way of telling them. Over time they warmed up to the idea when they saw how much they loved each other. Both Kim and Liz realized that if they fought them living together they would only rebel. Since Malik had met his father's family, both he and Gabrielle had started attending services with them and even convinced Liz to come with them sometimes. Seeing how much of a positive influence they had on each other made their living situation a little easier but they both wanted Malik and Gabrielle to understand that they did not condone it.

"Malik, I'm pregnant."

Malik fell back on the couch in shock. "What do you mean you're pregnant? I always use a condom."

"I know but their not one hundred percent effective, especially when you use the same one twice in one night."

"Ok, so how am I supposed to know that this baby is mine?"

Gabrielle looked at Malik in shock. Her eyes widened as her bottom lip trembled. She started crying uncontrollably. Malik had turned his head away knowing he had hurt Gabrielle. He knew that she wasn't having sex with anyone else but was so caught off guard that he didn't realize what he had said.

"Gabrielle, I'm…" Before he could recant his words Gabrielle ran into the bathroom and locked the door behind her. Malik ran after her trying to catch her before locked the door only to have the door slammed in his face. He placed his forehead on the door with his eyes closed.

"I'm sorry, I didn't mean it that way." The only response Malik got was the sound of Gabrielle throwing up. "Gabby, open the door. Are you okay?" Malik started banging on the door to their hallway bathroom hoping Gabrielle would open the door.

Gabrielle finally opened the bathroom door. She stood in the hallway looking at Malik as he was now sitting on the floor outside the door. She cut her eyes at him and went into the bedroom to lie down. Malik followed her and lay on the bed next to her, wrapping his arms around her stomach. He became so overwhelmed that tears began to form in the corner of his eyes. He couldn't believe he was going to be a dad. It was as if the thought of him reproducing a child was too much to consider. Malik's hidden fear was that he would be like his father. It had been three years since he met his father's family and he had yet to actually meet his father. Every time he came by the house Darnell was always busy doing something somewhere else with someone else. Darnell had started his own church so he did not see him on Sunday's when Malik and Gabrielle went to his grandfather's church.

"I'm scared Gabrielle, that's all."

"Just shut up and hold me Malik."

Malik held on tighter to Gabrielle as the tears began to roll down his cheek. His thoughts changed from him being a father to explaining to his mother that she was going to be a grandmother. This made Malik cry even more. He knew his mother would be disappointed in him. She wanted him to make sure he was able to do everything he wanted and go everywhere he wanted to go before he got married and had children. He had done so well with his woodwork that he had opened up a store in Georgia and has more orders than he could imagine. Because of this, it left little time for Malik to go anywhere. He had planned to take a break before years end so he could spend some much overdue time with his mother.

"When are we going to tell everyone Gabby."

"I don't know Malik. Are you sure you don't want to wait until we have a DNA test?"

"I said I was sorry. I was just in shock."

"So much shock the first thing you thought about was me cheating on you?"

"No, the first thing I thought was how in the world am I going to father a child when my own father wasn't there for me."

Gabrielle sat up and turned to face Malik. "You are not you're father. That coward won't even take the time to meet you!"

"Okay, I don't want to make you or the baby upset."

"I'm not upset, I'm just emotional."

"Are you sure you're pregnant?"

"Yes I'm sure. I went to the doctors a few days ago. I'm eight weeks. I was just waiting for the right time to tell you. I was afraid of how you would respond."

"Oh."

"Yes, oh."

"Ok. We have to tell everyone sooner than later. It might be easier to get everyone in a room together at the same time. That way they'll buffer their responses."

"You think that'll work?"

"We won't know until we find out."

"Well, when are we going to tell them?"

"Our graduation dinner. My mom's coming down with Greg for that weekend so it'll be perfect."

"I think I'm going to be sick again." Gabrielle jumped off the bed and ran into the master bathroom, this time leaving the door open. Malik instantly started feeling sick. He was temporarily distracted by the phone ringing. "I'll get it." He said.

Malik ran to get the cordless phone out the living room. "Hello."

"Hi Malik?"

"Yes, this is Malik. Who is this?"

"Darnell, your father. I've been meaning to call you but I've been so busy with the church I never seem to have a chance to call you."

"Mmm hmm." Malik could tell by his father's voice that he was lying.

"Listen, I know you're graduation is next Tuesday but I won't be able to make it. I have a three night conference to do next week and I'm leaving Tuesday morning to prepare for it."

"So that means you'll be back in time for the graduation party on Saturday right?"

"No son."

"Malik is fine."

"No, Malik I won't. The conference starts Thursday. Shannon and the kids will be there. You know your grandfather wouldn't miss it for the world. Anyway, I got you something and I wanted to give it to you in person but like I said, I won't be in town. Shannon will bring it to the graduation party for me. I'm sure you'll like it."

"Sure, well you enjoy your conference."

"Thanks. And Malik."

"Yeah."

"I'm very proud of the man you're becoming."

"Thank you sir. I have to go."

"Oh, ok. Good bye."

"Bye."

Gabrielle walked down the hall towards the living room with a damp rag on her forehead. "Who was that?"

"My father. He said he won't be able to make it to graduation or the party next week. He has a three day conference starting Thursday."

"But our graduation is Tuesday!" Gabrielle shook her head as she saw the look of disappointment on Malik's face.

"I know and apparently he knows too."

Graduation came sooner than Malik and Gabrielle thought it would. Gabrielle had been so sick the past few weeks that she had lost almost ten pounds. The doctor told her to take it easy and try to eat light meals throughout the day to prevent her from having an empty stomach. As Gabrielle walked down the aisle she became sad. She realized that her mother and father wouldn't see her graduate or ever get to meet their grandchild. Her eyes swelled with tears as she made her way to her seat. Malik sat a few seats from her and tried to get her attention to make sure she was okay.

He had been up with her the past few nights trying to get her to calm down enough to stop throwing up. The stress of them telling their families about the baby was becoming too much for Gabrielle so they decided to tell them after graduation instead of waiting until that weekend.

After the graduation ceremony was over Malik and Gabrielle met their families in the parking lot. Just before Malik could open his mouth to speak, Gabrielle ran over to the grass to throw up. Liz went to hold her hair out the way and Kim looked on in concern.

"I hope she doesn't have food poisoning. How long has she been like this Malik?"

"Um, a few weeks now."

"A few weeks?" Shannon chimed in. "I think we should get her to a doctor!"

"She's been to the doctor already." Malik said.

"Well what did they say Malik?" Kim asked in a stern and concerned voice.

"They said there's nothing they can really do, she just has to ride it out and try to eat small meals so she won't have an empty stomach."

"Well, I've never heard of a stomach virus lasting that long." Shannon said in an overly concerned tone.

"I've never heard of a doctor saying there's nothing they can do about it." Liz said as she walked back over with Gabrielle.

"You guys please." Danielle said as she looked at Malik. He had told his brother and sisters the night before so they could buffer their parent's reactions. Malik's eyes got real wide as he stared at his sister. "What Malik? You were going to tell them anyway."

"Tell us what?" Kim, Liz and Shannon said in unison.

"I'm pregnant." Gabrielle said as she fought back tears.

"You're what? Oh Father!" Liz said as she threw her hands in the air.

"Malik, is this true?" Kim asked with her hands on her hips.

"Yes mom. Gabrielle's pregnant." Malik said in low tone.

"Well I'll be…" Kim lashed.

"Ma!" Malik's eyes widened with embarrassment.

"What Malik? I told you both that if you do anything just don't have no baby right now! You're only twenty three for Christ's sake!" Kim was now yelling at both Malik and Gabrielle.

"Ma, don't use the Lord's name in vain." Malik was now yelling at his mother.

"What! Malik I will knock you into next week!" Kim threw her arm up to hit Malik but Greg grabbed her arm before she could hit him.

"Calm down Kim, not in the parking lot!" Greg yelled. He then turned to Malik and with a stern look said, "We'll deal with you at the house."

"We'll deal with both of you at the house!" Liz said.

"Gabrielle get in the car." Liz pointed to the limo that sat out in front of them.

"Get in Malik!" Kim said.

Shannon looked at Malik and shook her head in disappointment. She placed her hand on Kim's shoulder. Kim turned her head and calmed herself down for a moment.

"Shannon, thanks so much for coming. I'll be in contact with you to let you know about this weekend. We may forego the graduation party. So you can let Darnell know in case you guys wanted to make other plans." Kim and Shannon had a long conversation since Malik went to meet his family a few years earlier. They were both able to get past their issues with one another. They realized they were both caught in Darnell's lies and there was no need for the two of them to be nasty towards each other. Darnell was the problem and until he was ready to address everything, they maintained a mutual level of respect for each other.

"Thanks for letting me know Kim but Darnell's out of town until Monday so he wouldn't have made it anyway. I'm sure Danielle will keep me updated about the baby and congratulations Malik and Gabrielle. It was a beautiful ceremony." Shannon waived good bye to everyone glad that she didn't have to be apart of the baby conversation. She had almost forgotten about the gift Darnell had left for Malik. "Oh Kim, can you give this to Malik for me. It's from Darnell."

Kim took the card from Shannon and hugged her before she turned to get in the limousine. She shook her head as she closed the door.

Chapter Twenty Three

It had been three and a half months since Malik and Gabrielle had told everyone she was pregnant. Greg convinced Kim that she should be happy that their son was creating a very successful business. With the money his father had been sending him since he was a baby not being touched, Malik had a very nice nest egg to fall back on if business got slow. Even though Kim was not too excited at becoming a grandmother at forty four; she was excited that she didn't have to worry about her grandson wanting for anything.

Liz on the other hand, was overjoyed. It had taken her a little while to get over the shock of Gabrielle having a baby but once she saw the first ultrasound, her heart melted. She had changed one of her guest suites into a nursery for the baby. Most of Liz's time was spent working at the foundation she developed for her daughter's namesake, Victoria Holden. The decorating of the nursery preoccupied what little free time she had and kept her from thinking about the fact that she would never have her own biological grandchildren. She loved Gabrielle as if she were her own child and couldn't be happier that she was having a baby but there was still a part of her that longed to have her own grandchildren.

Malik and Gabrielle decided to design the furniture for the baby's room themselves. They decided not to move until they found a house they could agree on so they changed the second bedroom in their apartment to a nursery. Malik had already made a bassinet and was working on the dresser for the baby. His grandfather, Bishop Allen, had begun counseling the two of them once he found out Gabrielle was pregnant. He wanted them both to understand what a heavy responsibility raising a child was. He also wanted them to realize that they now had to make better decisions because they would soon have an extra life to consider.

They were just leaving a counseling session with Bishop Allen when Gabrielle got a severe sharp pain in her stomach. She thought it was just the baby kicking her until she felt it again. This time the pain was so bad she doubled over grabbing her stomach. Malik sat her down on the bench outside Bishop Allen's office and went to get his grandfather. By the time he came back with his grandfather Gabrielle was on the floor with a small puddle of fluid surrounding her. Bishop Allen told Malik to call an ambulance and he began to pray for Gabrielle and the baby.

It took fifteen minutes for the ambulance to arrive and another twenty to get to the emergency room. The paramedic informed Gabrielle that she was in labor but not to panic. When the ambulance arrived at the emergency room, Liz and Shannon were in the lobby waiting for them. The paramedics rushed passed them with Gabrielle on a gurney into the double doors at the end of the hallway. Liz and Shannon followed them but were stopped at the doors to the trauma center.

"I'm her mother." Liz said.

The nurse signaled her hand to let Liz in. Liz turned back around before the door closed. She looked at Shannon and told her to call Kim to let he know what was happening. Liz ran down the hall to the room where they took Gabrielle and grabbed Malik.

"What happened Malik?"

"I don't know. We were just finishing up a session with granddad and she started flinching. I went to get my granddad. A few minutes later she was on the floor and there was a puddle of brown fluid around her. I don't know if she was bleeding or what but we called the ambulance and the paramedic said she was in labor. The doctor's going to try to stop it. I need to call my mom."

"Shannon's calling her right now."

"God mommy!" Gabrielle yelled out.

"I'm right here baby. So is Malik." Liz said as she grabbed Gabrielle's right hand and held it tight.

Malik went to Gabrielle's other side and held her left hand. The doctor came in and began to check to see if Gabrielle's cervix had dilated. He had the nurse put a monitor on Gabrielle's stomach to monitor the baby's heart rate. The nurse moved the monitor around her stomach for a while trying to find a heart beat. She pulled the doctor to the side and whispered in his ear. The doctor came back with a heart rate monitor in his hand and began to try and find the baby's heart beat. The nurse left out the room for a few minutes returning with an ultrasound machine. She turned the machine on and set it up with the screen facing away from Gabrielle, Malik and Liz. The doctor began to rub the monitor for the ultrasound machine across Gabrielle's stomach for a few moments. He said absolutely nothing.

Liz broke the silence. "What's going on doctor?"

The doctor turned the machine off. He looked at Liz with a serious face. "I need to run some tests. Gabrielle, I am going to take a sample of the fluid and I will be back shortly."

Gabrielle was in severe pain at this point and was crying uncontrollably.

"Can't you give her something for the pain?"

"We will." The doctor called out to the nurse to follow him in the hallway of the ER.

"It's going to be ok Gabby." Malik said as Gabrielle squeezed his hand.

The doctor came back moments later with another doctor. "Gabrielle, this is Dr. Johnson. He's an ultrasonic specialist. We seem to be having trouble finding the baby's heart rate so he is going to insert an internal monitor to your cervix so that we can make sure the baby's heart rate is ok. I am having a few tests run on your amniotic fluid to determine why you're water broke."

"My water broke? I'm only six months pregnant. It's not time."

"Gabrielle, I need you to stay as calm as you can. The anesthesiologist is going to give you an epidural to slow down the contractions until we can determine what further steps need to be taken."

"See baby, it's going to be alright." Liz said as she patted Gabrielle's hand.

Dr. Johnson inserted the fetal heart monitor and hooked it up to the monitor next to Gabrielle's hospital bed. He turned the machine on and hit the record button so that the machine could print the heart rhythm and the contraction frequency. He stood and looked for a while at the print out, went over to the ER doctor and showed him what he found. They both looked at each other then at Gabrielle.

Dr. Johnson and the ER doctor walked out the room and began to talk in the hallway. Dr. Johnson came back in and stood next to Liz. "Gabrielle, I'm afraid your baby does not have a heart beat."

"What? I'm in labor." Gabrielle said in between pants. The needle for the epidural had just been inserted in her back but had not taken affect yet. "I'm in labor, so my baby does have a heart beat."

"What you're experiencing right now is labor. You're cervix is readying itself for you to push the baby out. I need you to relax. I'm going to check to see how much you have dilated."

"Dr. Johnson there must be some mistake. We were just at the doctors a few days ago and they said everything was fine. The baby is fine. There must be something wrong with the machines. Are they plugged in?" Malik was yelling at Dr. Johnson to stop himself from crying.

"I'm sorry sir but there's nothing else we can do at this point but help her deliver this baby. I will let you know when to start pushing once I see how far you've dilated."

'I'm not pushing my baby out! It's not time! It's not time. God mommy, tell them it's not time!"

Liz was holding on to Gabrielle's hand as tight as she could. She was overwhelmed by everything. She looked at Dr. Johnson with a stern face. "We want a second opinion."

"Ma'am I am the second opinion."

"Well then we need a third." Malik yelled.

"Fine, we will see if we can get your obstetrician in. In the meantime, please let me check to see how far dilated you are."

Gabrielle relaxed her legs enough for Dr. Johnson to examine her. He stood up and looked Gabrielle in the eyes. "You're fifty percent effaced and dilated six centimeters. I will see who I can get in here but you need to prepare yourself to push ma'am."

Gabrielle started crying all over again. The epidural had kicked in but now she was frightened.

Bishop Allen had called Gabrielle's obstetrician once he got off the phone with the hospital and informed Dr. Foyes of the situation. She was already in the hospital and came down to the ER as soon as she had heard that Gabrielle had arrived. Dr Foyes walked through the doorway after she was updated of the situation.

"Dr. Foyes! Please tell these doctor's that their wrong. There's nothing wrong with my baby!"

"Hi Gabrielle. Let me take a look here and I will let you know what the situation is." Dr. Foyes checked Gabrielle's cervix. She them took the external fetal heart monitor and began to rub it across Gabrielle's stomach. She took out her stethoscope and used that to trace the heart rate but heard nothing.

She looked at Gabrielle and then at Malik. "I'm sorry Gabrielle. There's nothing else we can do. Your baby has no heart rate."

"No!" Gabrielle screamed at the top of her lungs.

Malik stood up and wrapped his arms around Gabrielle. He was rocking back and forth with a flood of tears falling from his eyes. Liz got up to speak with Dr. Foyes to avoid from crying herself.

"Will you be able to tell what happened? This makes no sense! She hasn't had any complications at all during her pregnancy outside of her morning sickness. We need answers Dr. Foyes."

"And I will try to get you those answers however, right now, we need to have Gabrielle deliver the fetus so that it does not cause internal damage. From the tests, it looks like she has been bleeding internally for a few weeks. She might get an infection if she does not deliver this baby soon. That's if she already doesn't have one. I need you to work with me to calm her down enough to deliver the baby."

Liz shut her eyes as hard as she could to avoid them from swelling up with tears. She then turned around and walked back into the emergency room followed by Dr. Foyes.

"Gabby honey, I know you're upset right now but we need you to be strong. Dr. Foyes believes you might have an infection and they need to deliver the baby so that it doesn't harm you."

Liz walked over to Malik and placed her hands on his shoulders. "Malik, I need you to let go."

"No, this is not happening. We just decided on the colors for the wall in the nursery. I'm making his dresser. It's almost done."

Liz let go off Malik's shoulders. She realized she couldn't handle this alone. She walked out to the waiting area of the emergency room to find Shannon. As Liz walked over to Shannon, she tried to keep herself composed as much as she could. "I need your help."

"I contacted Kim. She said she would get her as soon as possible the next flight that she could get on leaves in a half an hour. How's the baby? How's Gabrielle?"

"The baby's dead." Liz said in a faint voice. "They couldn't find a heart rate. Dr. Foyes said that Gabrielle has been internally bleeding for at least a few weeks and since their not sure how long the baby hasn't had a heart beat they need to do an emergency delivery. They want her to push, they want her to push." Liz couldn't hold it in any longer. She felt faint. Shannon grabbed her by her shoulders and started praying for God to give them all strength.

"Ok Liz. Ok. Have a seat here. I'm going to call Malik's grandfather to update him and see if he can get here as soon as possible. Is there anyone else you need me to call?"

Liz just sat in the chair staring out the window. Shannon tapped her left knee startling her. Liz shook her head to come out the trance she was in. "She doesn't deserve this. Neither of them does. They've been working so hard to make sure they were doing what was best for the baby." Liz sighed long and hard.

Shannon took out her phone and called Bishop Davis to inform him of what was going on. She walked away from Liz so that she wouldn't upset her anymore than she already was. As Shannon ended the call, Liz walked up behind her.

"What did Bishop Davis say?"

"He'll be here in fifteen minutes. He was already headed here. He just needed to make sure someone could lock the church up for him."

"Ok, I'm going to check on Gabrielle and Malik. Let Bishop know we're in room 313."

"Ok, I will."

Liz walked back towards the double doors that led to the trauma center.

"Liz!"

She turned around to find Shannon standing in the main lobby. Shannon ran up to Liz and gave her a big hug. "I'm sorry. Tell them I'm sorry."

"I will Shannon. Thank you. You've been very helpful."

As Liz walked back into the room, Malik and Gabrielle were in the same position they were when she had left them. Liz walked over and rubbed Malik's back. The nurses had left them alone to give them some time to deal with the situation.

"Malik, your mothers on her way. She should be here in a few hours. Bishop Davis is on his way here as well."

"Does my mom know?"

"No honey, I thought it was best to wait until she got here."

"Where's Ms. Shannon? Did she leave?"

"She's in the waiting area"

Malik let go of Gabrielle and sat back down in the chair next to her. She grabbed his hand before he could pull it away from her. Malik looked into Gabrielle's eyes. He had never felt so helpless before. He knew there was nothing to make this situation better. Malik started praying while he held Gabrielle's hand.

"Dear God, please help us deal with this hurt. Let there be no permanent damage Lord. I know you are a healer so please heal our hearts right now God. Please heal our minds so that this doesn't drive us crazy. There has to be a reason why you allowed this to happen so just help us to understand so that we don't become angry. Because right now, I'm hurting so bad Lord!" He had begun sobbing while he was praying. "I wanted a chance to prove that I could be a good father. Lord please help Gabrielle to be strong. She has to do something right now that seems unfair. She has to deliver a baby we'll never see breath or smile or even cry. Help me to help her through this. Help us to make it through this." Malik began crying uncontrollably.

Bishop Davis walked in at that moment and went to Malik's side. He picked Malik up and hugged him as tight as he could. "It's going to be ok son."

Dr. Foyes had been monitoring Gabrielle from the nurse's station. She could see that Gabrielle was having contractions every thirty five to forty seconds. She came back in the room once it looked like everyone was a lot calmer.

"Gabrielle, we're going to lower the dosage of your epidural so that you can feel when to push. I know this is going to be hard but you have a lot of support here to help you through this."

Gabrielle shook her head as tears rolled down her cheeks. She was in shock and denial at the same time. She took a few deep breathes and tried to relax as much as she could. She felt a warm feeling come over her body as if someone was lying right beside her in the hospital bed. She knew it was the Holy Spirit and a calmness came over her.

A few minutes later Gabrielle began to feel a tightness on her stomach and felt the urge to push. "I need to push. I have to push Dr. Foyes."

"Ok, that's good. Just let me check you're cervix again. Yes, you're ready. Now on the next contraction I want you to push."

Chapter Twenty Four

Kim knocked on Malik and Gabrielle's bedroom door. She didn't get an answer so she slowly opened the door and peeked in. Malik was sprawled out across the bed sleep. Gabrielle had been at the mansion since she had gotten out of the hospital. They had a small ceremony for the baby on the mansion grounds and buried Malik Jr. in the cemetery where Gabrielle's parents were buried. Malik stayed for a few nights but couldn't handle Gabrielle shutting him out like she was. They had not spoken to each other since the memorial service. Kim and Liz thought it would be best for the two of them to spend some time apart to get past the loss of their child.

"Sweetie you have to eat something."

Malik covered his head with a pillow and made a growling sound. Kim walked over and sat on the edge of the bed. She patted Malik's leg. She had never felt so helpless. She didn't know what to say to her son to make him feel better. Kim looked around the messy bedroom. "You know you should really clean up in here before Gabrielle comes home. It's a mess."

"She's not coming back here."

"Oh Malik, stop being so dramatic! How do you know she's not coming back home?"

"Because she told me she wasn't."

"Well when did she say that? You guys haven't spoken in weeks."

"I called her last week. She said that losing a baby was a sign we shouldn't be together and we would be fools not to pay attention to it."

"Well, what would give her an idea like that? Better yet, who would give her an idea like that? Malik, that doesn't make any sense. She had no control over what happened. There was no way to know the pills she was taking for morning sickness would have such an adverse affect on the baby."

"Ma, I'm just telling you what she said. She said it was her fault she lost the baby. She shouldn't have taken those pills the doctor gave her for morning sickness. She thinks they're what killed the baby and if she had been a strong enough mother she would've been able to handle the morning sickness without having to take pills."

"I don't want to hear anymore of this. I'm calling Liz."

"Ma, what's done is done. Besides we were too young to be so serious. I mean we barely got to enjoy college. We spent all of our time with each other and missed out on some great opportunities."

"Malik, you're both upset and just need some time."

"Well, we'll have plenty of it now."

"I'm calling Liz. I'll be back"

"She's not there. Neither one of them are. They should be in Portugal by now."

"Portugal? What's in Portugal?"

"I don't know. I just know that's where they are."

Malik rolled off of the bed planting his feet onto the floor. He walked past his mother into the master bathroom and shut the door. Kim looked at the bathroom door shaking her head. She had to figure out a way to fix this but didn't know how. Kim knew what she had to do. "Malik, I'm going to run a few errands and pick up some dinner. I'll be back" Kim waited a moment to see if she would get a response from Malik before she grabbed her purse and headed out the door.

Kim pulled up to Darnell's church twenty minutes later. She slammed the car door shut to release some of her frustration before she entered the church. God had done nothing wrong to her but God's servant had. She did not want to disrespect the church with what she had to say but she had no choice.

Kim walked into the sanctuary and found her way to the back where the Pastor's office was located. She knocked on the cracked door waiting for a response before she entered.

"Come in."

Kim opened the doorway to see Darnell sitting behind a long cherry finished desk looking up at her.

"May I help you ma'am."

"It figures you wouldn't recognize me!"

"I'm sorry, you do look familiar but your name seems to slip my mind."

"Maybe the name Malik Simms can refresh your memory."

Darnell leaned back in his chair with a dumb look on his face. "How do you know Malik?"

"He's my son." Kim said solemnly.

"Kim." Darnell said in a sullen voice.

"Yes Darnell, it's me." Kim felt the heat on her face which meant it was completely red. "I just want to know one thing. How is it that your son can live less than an hour from you for years and you make not one iota of an effort to see him? You've been given the opportunity of a lifetime and instead you choose to be a coward just like you were when you were younger and hide with your head tucked between your legs!"

"Kim, please don't come in here and become indignant with me! I'm not the one that got pregnant and decided to tell me at the last and I do mean very last minute! You told me you were on birth control!"

"You were married you son of a bitch! MARRIED" Kim began yelling as she slammed the door and walked closer to Darnell's desk. She looked up at the ceiling as she inhaled and exhaled deeply. The last thing she wanted was to turn this into a meeting about their past. Their son needed his father. She knew there was a bond that Malik and Greg would never be able to have and only Darnell could give him the validation he desperately needed.

Darnell could see the frustration Kim had. He folded his arms on the desk determined to keep his composure.

"I'm sorry." Kim said shaking her head. "That's not why I'm here. I made sure you knew how I felt twenty four years ago. Your son needs you Darnell."

"I'm not sure he even wants to see me. I don't want to see me sometimes."

"He lost his fight somewhere Darnell. He used to fight for everything. He had this drive about him that I was so envious of because I know I hadn't given it to him. He isn't working and he's losing business left and right. He needs you Darnell."

"What would you like me to do Kim? Go over there and give him a great big hug and tell him everything's going to work out? It's not like he's one of my members that I have a degree of separation from. I'm sure when he looks at me all he sees is disappointment. Besides, my father…"

"Your father what? Your father has stood in the gap for you long enough. He's not you Darnell. He's not you!"

"Listen Kim, it's not that I haven't wanted to sit down and talk to Malik. I have just been busy with the church."

"You know that's the most straight forward thing you've said Darnell. You're correct; you have been busy with the church." Kim looked at Darnell with a look of pity on her face. "Four years Darnell. He's been here four years. Can you imagine how Malik must feel? You've known where he was his entire life and he's still not worth enough for you to take time out of your so busy schedule to reach out to your son. He's your son Darnell your son who just lost his own son and can't cope with it."

"Kim, I just."

Kim turned her back to Darnell to walk out the door. She stopped in the doorway, closed her eyes and turned back around. "Do you know when Malik found out he was having a son, the first thing he said was that he would make sure his son knew how important his life was everyday. Some times Darnell, being too busy to say a simple I love you or hello could mean more than you know."

Kim walked out the door hoping she had made her point.

Chapter Twenty Five

Malik drove up the driveway to the cemetery where his son was buried. He parked and walked up the grassy hill to his tomb stone. There was someone already knelt down at the grave with their head down. As he got closer he recognized the silhouette of Gabrielle. Malik walked up beside her and placed his hand on her shoulder. Gabrielle jumped up startled by his touch. It had been a month since they buried their son.

"I thought you were in Portugal?"

"I couldn't calm down enough to get on the plane."

Malik knelt beside Gabrielle and they sat there crying silently not speaking a word. Malik finally turned to Gabrielle and waited for her to look at him.

"I miss you Gabrielle. This is hard for me too you know."

"Malik, I know it is. I miss you too."

Malik wrapped his arm around Gabrielle's waste and she rested her head on his left shoulder. They stayed that way in silence for a few more minutes.

"I'm sorry I lost the baby Malik. Even though you don't say it, I know you're disappointed in me. I mean what kind of woman can't carry a baby to term?"

"Gabby, it's not your fault. I don't know how many different ways I can say it but it's not your fault. The doctor said there was no way for you to know that the baby's heart had a defect. He was a feisty little thing. They couldn't even get a good ultrasound picture of him because he moved so much."

"He's must've gotten that from you." Gabrielle started laughing and then began crying on Malik's shoulder. Malik fought back his tears. He was trying his best to be strong but he felt so defeated. Deep down inside, Malik believed that it just wasn't meant for him to have children and that's why Gabrielle lost the baby.

"Yeah, he must have."

"Malik, don't think I don't love you because I do. From that day we met in the dorms on campus I've felt like we had this crazy connection that no one could shake. It's like we're supposed to be in each others lives. I just don't know if it was just to be friends and we made more of it than it was supposed to be. I mean who would've thought that a few weeks after meeting each other you'd be donating an organ to me? Maybe that was why God brought us together and that was supposed to be it. I know we'll always be apart of each other's lives, we have no choice. We'd probably stalk each other if we weren't." They both giggled.

"Where is all this coming from? I know it's been hard on both of us losing the baby but I always felt if we worked together we could get through anything. I don't want to loose you too!" Malik began to feel angry, as if Gabrielle was punishing him for something neither one of them had control over.

Gabrielle placed her hand inside Malik's. "I'm not your father Malik. I couldn't imagine not being a part of your life. I'm just saying that maybe we need to just take a step back. Can you understand that? It's hard for me to think about what we lost and not feel like it was a sign that maybe we weren't ready for what we thought we were."

"I understand Gabby. I don't like it but I understand. And for the record, yes, I would definitely stalk you."

Gabrielle poked Malik in the stomach, "You'd better! I need someone to look out for me!"

"Can you at least come back home? I don't want you to be by yourself and my mom is going back home in a few days. To be honest with you, I don't want to be by myself either. We need to pack up the nursery stuff anyway and I can't do it alone Gabby, I need you."

"Let me think about it. Malik losing Malik Jr. took a lot out of me. I haven't been back to the house since I went to the hospital. I'm not sure I'm strong enough to deal with that yet."

"I'll be there Gabby. We'll deal with it together."

"Thank you for being you Malik. You don't know how much strength you give me."

"You don't know how much strength you've given me."

Malik and Gabby stood at the grave site for a few more minutes without speaking. Malik was finally able to accept that it was over between them but was determined to keep Gabrielle in his life, one way or another. They walked away from the headstone for Malik Simms Jr. accepting one life had ended too soon and two lives were about to begin again.

Chapter Twenty Six

"Madame, Madame." A woman stood in front of Liz and broke her out of her trance.

"Yes. Do you speak English?" Liz asked. She did not speak Portuguese at all and had left her translation book at the hotel.

"Yes, yes I do." The woman answered as she walked closer to Liz.

Liz sat in the chair trying to gather her thoughts.

"How can I help you Madame?"

"I'm looking for records of properties in Lisbon called Loures. It would be under the name of Holden."

"Do you mean the Holden Estates?"

"I believe so. I'm sorry I've never actually been there but I am sure that it is in Loures."

"Si, si. I know the place."

"Is there anyone still living there?"

"Ah, I can not say. I have never been. I've only seen pictures. It is private property. I don't know how close you'll get."

"I think I'll be able to get pretty close. Is there a map I can copy or buy to get there?"

"Yes. We have maps you can copy. Like I said Madame, it is private property."

"I understand. May I please get a copy of the map?"

An hour later, Liz was in the limo headed to the Holden Estates in Loures, Lisbon. Her driver was familiar with the estate and didn't need the map she had printed. Liz followed the roads they travelled on the map and became very nervous as she eventually was able to see the estate in the far off distance.

She was able to find birth records for a child born around the time frame that Cynthia had left to go to Portugal. Her name was Zeta Dillon born twenty seven years prior. There was no record of a death certificate on file.

As they pulled up to the gate of the property, Liz leaned forward to look out the front window. She could see that the grounds were still well kept which meant that there was still someone living on the property.

"Hola, que te ayudo?" Liz heard the voice of a young woman through the intercom at the gate. She pulled her Spanish dictionary out of her Prada bag and tried to skim through the pages to figure out what the person on the intercom was saying.

The driver lowered his sunglasses as he turned around to look at Liz. "She said hello, how can she help you."

"Oh, ok."

Liz rolled her window down and pushed the button on the intercom. "Me llamo es Liz. Elizabeth Holden. Busco Senora Sara Holden? Soy de niece?"

"Hablas Ingles?"

"Uh. Muy bien."

The driver lowered his sunglasses as he turned around again. "She said do you speak English Madame."

"Oh, si. Yes, I do. Do you speak English?"

"Yes, I do. Did you say you're Sarah Holden's niece?"

"Yes, my husband, Mark was her nephew. I came on vacation and wanted to see her before I left." Liz was lying to get in the gate. She figured she could ask all questions once she got inside.

"She's my grandmother."

There was silence for what seemed like ten minutes before the gate opened. As the car pulled up the driveway to the cul de sac, Liz could see a beautiful young woman standing on the porch. The car stopped at the front door and the driver got out letting Liz out of the car.

Liz saw a resemblance in the young woman that almost shocked her. She looked exactly like Cyndi did when she was younger. The only difference was that she had a glow about her that Cyndi never had.

Liz walked up to the young lady and put her hand out to shake hers. "Hi, I'm Liz."

"Hello, I'm Zeta Dillon. My grandmother is inside. She said she was expecting you."

Liz looked slightly confused. She had no idea how Aunt Sara could have known she was coming.

"Lizzie? Is that you?" said a voice far off down the hall. Liz could see an elderly woman in a wheel chair being rolled toward them. "I haven't seen you since you married my nephew almost fifteen years ago. You still look as lovely as you did on your wedding day."

"So do you Aunt Sara." Liz smiled as she walked closer to Aunt Sara to give her a hug.

"Aunt Sara, how did you know I was coming? I wanted it to be a surprise."

"I've been waiting on you to come for years honey." Aunt Sara had lived in Portugal for over forty years but she still had her southern accent. It was the one thing she promised she'd never give up when she moved across the ocean.

Sara nodded her head at Zeta who nodded back and walked down the hall toward the stair case. "It was nice to meet you Aunt Liz."

"Yes, it was a pleasure to meet you too Zeta."

"Come with me Liz," Aunt Sara said as she pointed her right hand towards the family room, "We have a lot to discuss."

"Yes, we do."

"Marco, please bring us some tea." Aunt Sara waited for Marco to walk out of hearing distance before she began to speak. "So I'm assuming Cyndi finally told you?"

"Yes, I just don't understand Aunt Sara. Why keep such a secret for so long? Do you realize how much this has been eating away at her? She's been drinking for years and I just thought it was because she was a spoiled brat who never wanted to grow up."

Aunt Sara nodded her head as she closed her eyes. "I warned her mother that this would not be a good situation. But my niece being who she was always thought she knew what was best for her children."

"Did Mark know? I would think he would've told me if he knew."

"Not even her own child knows honey."

"You mean Zeta has no idea!"

Aunt Sara's eyes widened. "I see you've done your research." She sighed deeply before she began to speak again. "The plan was to bring Cyndi here once she was near the end of her second trimester. That way she wouldn't miss too much school and we would tell everyone that she was just very ill and needed a change of scenery. She was to give birth to the baby and return home a week later fully recovered from her illness. The baby was to immediately be given up for adoption and Cyndi would never see her again."

"I don't understand. Isn't that what happened? How did she end up here?"

"When Cyndi went into labor it was the middle of the winter. There was a bad storm and the doctor couldn't get to the road until the morning. I had to deliver the baby and needless to say there were complications. The baby had an infection and the doctor thought it would be best to wait until she was better before sending her to her adopted family,"

"So the baby was still in the house while Cyndi was here?"

"No, her mother had them flown back the next day. They went to their house in the Hamptons for a few weeks. Cyndi was still in shock about the whole situation and had even run out to the wood cabin on the back of the property looking for the baby in the middle of the night. Jackie thought it would be best to wait until Cyndi was a little calmer before returning home. I could tell that it was too overwhelming for her. She just wanted to hold her baby and we denied her of that."

"I still have one issue that doesn't make sense. Why is Zeta here now? Or has she been here all along?"

"Like I said, the doctor couldn't make it to the house until the morning because of the snow. Alicia took the baby to her cottage for the night. She had just stopped nursing her son so she was able to nurse the baby. When the doctor came the next afternoon, Alicia couldn't seem to part with the baby."

"Alicia is your daughter? I remember meeting her a few times but that was before Mark and I were married."

"Yes, she was. She passed away ten years ago. Alicia kept the baby."

"Zeta Dillon? Was that the baby's name?"

"Yes, the young woman that greeted you at the door is Zeta. She's Cynthia's child."

Liz leaned forward and put her hands on her head. She was overwhelmed. She felt Aunt Sara's hand on her back. Liz shook her head in her hands. "Aunt Sara, why? When Cynthia told me about the baby, she almost went crazy! I had never seen her like that before. I lost my best friend years ago because of something she had no control over?"

"Liz, I was not aware of anything until a few weeks before Jackie and Cyndi came to Portugal. Jackie was in a panic. She had just found out her fifteen year old daughter was pregnant and she panicked. She didn't want James to find out. She knew it would kill him to know his baby girl was having a baby. Jackie asked for my help."

"Aunt Sara, do you remember my wedding?"

"I remember."

"Do you remember her walking on the table and knocking over the cake? She was drunk! She has been like that for almost half her life. Burying this secret for what?"

"Liz, I wish there was something I could've done but I had to respect her mother's wishes."

"What about Cyndi's wishes? This was her life! Her child! What right did any of you have to make a decision like that for her?"

"Liz, please calm down. I will talk to Cyndi myself. Explain everything to her. Just give me some time to get my thoughts together. Jackie's gone. Alicia's gone. I've bore this by myself for fifteen years."

"Aunt Sara, this has been a secret for twenty seven years. You've had enough time to think about this. You've seen Zeta everyday of her life. This web of secrets and lies has to stop! Cynthia's life depends on it and Zeta deserves the truth."

Chapter Twenty Seven

Liz rode back to her hotel room thinking about Cynthia, Zeta and Gabrielle. She had become frustrated by all of the secrets she'd kept in her life; secrets of others and her own secrets. She began to get a headache just thinking about how much one secret affected the life of her best friend. Her frustration made her angry. Liz tried to think of a way to help Cyndi get back all the years of her life she missed out on because of a secret that destroyed her life. Tears filled her eyes as she became enraged. She could no longer see beyond the tears or her own frustration. Liz felt the urge to pray but couldn't mouth the words to speak or get the sound to come out.

Completely overwhelmed she pulled up to the hotel she was staying at and opened the door without looking. As she jumped out of the car she stood face to face with Zeta.

"Is it true?" Zeta asked.

Liz looked dumbfounded for what seemed like an eternity. Zeta's eyes were filled with tears. Her eyes were red and she was shaking. Liz couldn't think of anything else to do but hug her. Zeta cried in her shoulder as they got back into the car. Liz rubbed Zeta's back until she calmed down.

"Zeta, how did you know where I was?" Liz asked in confusion.

"I followed you on my scooter. I'm surprised you didn't see me behind you. I heard you talking to abuela and I knew she wouldn't tell me the truth. She has been hiding things from me my whole life."

"I'm so sorry you had to find out this way." Liz hugged her again.

"For one in my life, I just want the truth." Zeta shook her head and began crying again.

Liz grabbed Zeta and hugged her again. "We'll work through this Zeta."

"I want to meet her, my mother, I want to meet her."

"Zeta, honey, lets take this one step at a time. She doesn't even know you're alive and believe it or not, you've already met her years ago. You were very young and probably don't remember it. We all thought you were Zachary's twin."

"So did I, oh my god I have to tell him. He has to know."

"Zeta, I need you to promise me something. Promise me you won't talk to Zack until we figure this out. We all need to sit down and talk this through, together. I have to go back home but I will be coming back in a few weeks. We will all sit down and talk then. Okay?"

Zeta shook her head yes.

Liz held out a tissue for Zeta. She then grabbed one for herself and wiped her eyes as she laughed.

Zeta had a confused look on her face as she spoke to Liz. "What's so funny?"

"You know when I came here; I thought my major problem was going to be translating everything to Spanish. Then I realized everyone speaks Portuguese! I was just thinking about how hard it was for me to even figure out how to say the words."

Liz chuckled lightly and realized Zeta wasn't laughing at all or even smiling.

"I'm really sorry that you found out like this Zeta." Liz straightened her face up and turned to face Zeta. "I promise you that you'll meet your real mother."

"Can I ask you something?" Zeta hesitated as she continued to speak. "What her name? My mom, what's her name?"

"It's Cynthia Holden. We call her Cyndi for short. I have a picture of her do you want to see it?"

"Yes, please."

Liz pulled an old picture of Cyndi that she kept in her wallet. "This was right before your cousin Mark and my wedding." Liz handed Zeta a photo of Cyndi wearing a lavender maid of honor dress. She was standing in the back yard of her parents house in front of the awning built for the wedding.

"She's beautiful."

"Yes she is. Zeta, I know this is a lot to take in for one day. I don't want you to let Aunt Sara know you know who you're real mother is. It's a lot I'm asking you but I need to talk to Cyndi before Aunt Sara gets in contact with her. Promise me you won't say anything."

Zeta closed her eyes to stop the tears from flowing again. She looked up at Liz with a look of pity on her face. "I promise. Can I at least keep the picture?"

"Sure, sure." Liz pushed the photo in Zeta's hand. "My flight leaves in a few hours. Like I said, I'll be back in a few weeks. If Aunt Sara mentions anything to you just pretend you never knew anything."

Chapter Twenty Eight

Liz arrived back in Atlanta a few days later feeling completely confused. She needed to talk to Cynthia but didn't think in her current state she could handle all of that information at one time. Her thoughts then turned to Gabrielle and she remembered that Gabrielle had no idea that Hernando was not her father. As the limo drove her up to the estate, Liz became more frustrated than she had ever been in her entire life. So many lies and secrets that affected the people she knew and loved and she couldn't take it anymore.

Liz walked into the house and went straight to her study. She picked up the phone and called the bank. She needed to get the letter Lydia left for Gabrielle; it was time Gabrielle knew the truth. As she spoke with the bank representative, she tried to remember the name of the woman that had come to see her and Lydia so many years ago. "Was it Trina? Tracy? What was that woman's name?" Liz slammed her hand down on her desk so hard that she knocked the book that sat on the end over. As she bent down to pick it up, she found an old business card on the floor. It read Trisha Johnson at the top. Liz hung the phone up on the bank and called the number on the card. She was hoping Trisha still had the same number after all of these years.

"Hello." Said a female voice on the other side of Liz's receiver.

"Hello, I'm trying to reach Trisha Johnson?" Liz said in a shaky voice.

"I'm sorry but she no longer works here." The voice said.

"Oh, forgive me, I had her business card from years ago and I was stretching out on a limb to hope she still had the same number. Do you have any other contact information for her? I'm a former acquaintance of hers and I would love to catch up with her." Liz embellished because she thought that was the only way she would get the information she needed.

"Oh yes, well since she moved to California, she's had the same number. I can give you her office number." The woman said in a nonchalant voice.

"Oh that would be great!" Liz tried her best to mask her excitement. She wrote down the number and dialed it as soon as she hung up with the woman.

The phone rang three times and Liz wondered if it was too early to call. She couldn't remember how many hours the west coast was behind the east coast. As she was about to hang up on the fourth ring, she heard a voice on the line. "Hi, is this Trisha Johnson?"

"Yes this is she, who am I speaking with?"

Liz had not thought of what she would say to Trisha and paused for a moment.

"Hello? Hello? Is anyone there?" Trisha asked in a confused tone.

"Yes, I'm sorry. I hadn't thought about what I would say to you before I called. You might not remember me but my name is Elizabeth Holden. I was Elizabeth Williams when I met you. My best friend Lydia, I mean Lucida was. Ok, this is harder than I thought. I'm sorry." Liz shook her head because she knew she sounded like an idiot calling this woman and not event knowing why she was calling her.

"I remember you. You were the feisty friend who threw me out of the house." Trisha was slightly chuckling on the other end of the receiver.

"Yes, that was me. I'm sorry, I had your business card and I called the number and got your information from the office. I just need a little help with something. Lydia died ten years ago and I have been helping to raise her daughter, Gabrielle since then. Her stepfather died not too long ago and now I'm left with the responsibility of telling Gabrielle that the man she thought was her father wasn't her father." Liz paused to sigh and try to figure out how to ask the question she had avoided for years.

"You want to know who her father is because you never talked about it with Lydia." Trisha said in a surprisingly calm voice.

"Yes, how did you know?" Liz asked confusingly

"Not long after I met with Lydia, she contacted me. She said that she had her husband sign Gabrielle's birth certificate when she was born and did not want to create more of a hassle for herself or her daughter because someone else's name was on the birth certificate. She didn't want the money and thought that if Gabrielle's real father's name wasn't on the birth certificate then she wouldn't have to ever worry about her daughter finding out about her past. I told her that regardless of whose name was on the birth certificate, if Darnell was indeed the father, he wanted to provide for Gabrielle."

"I'm sorry did you say Darnell?" Liz fell back in her chair as her heart began to race.

"Yes, Gabrielle's father's name is Darnell Allen. He lives in the suburbs of Atlanta and is a pastor of a church there called…"

"Ebenezer Second Baptist Church?" Liz said as she struggled to breathe.

"Yes, how did you know? Lydia said she wanted to keep that information confidential until Gabrielle was twenty four" Trisha asked in concern.

"Because, because. I think I'm going to be sick." Liz placed the phone on her chest as she tried to calm her heart rate. She began sweating and stood up to gain her composure. She could hear Trisha yelling on the phone. Liz placed the receiver back to her ear and spoke in a soft tone. "Gabrielle has already met her father and her brothers and sisters. I didn't know they were who they were. And Malik! Oh God! This is not happening!"

"How do you know about Malik?" Trisha asked in complete confusion.

"Because Malik went to Clark Atlanta University where he met Gabrielle and they had a child together." Liz said in a weak voice.

"What? I don't understand how this could happen! You mean they didn't know they were brother and sister? I am so sorry this happened! I wish there was something I could do to fix this." Trisha was shaking her head and her heart had begun racing as well. She grabbed a notepad from her desk. "Liz, let me get your information. I know this is going to be tough for you to explain to both of them and it's not fair for you to have to do this yourself. I'm going to get in contact with Bishop Allen and Shannon, Darnell's wife…"

"You don't have to do that, we've been going to Bishop Allen's church for a few years now. I can't believe this. This is too much for me to take in right now."

"Liz you have to know that I had no idea this would happen. I mean what are the odds of them both going to the same school. I am truly sorry. I feel almost responsible. Darnell was my responsibility and I just let him spread his wild oats like a teenager!" Trisha had begun to speak in an embarrassed tone.

"This isn't your fault at all Trisha. I'm sorry you're in the middle of this as much as I am." Liz shook her head and gathered her thoughts. She gave Trisha her cell number and address. They talked for a few more moments and Liz promised to keep her up to date as to what happened once Gabrielle and Malik were told that they were siblings.

Chapter Twenty Nine

Liz grabbed her butterfly stationary and began to write a letter to Malik, Gabrielle, Cynthia and Darnell. She didn't know how she would be able to release everything she knew face to face without breaking down. She could not stop the pounding in her heart as she wrote. After she finished the letter to each of them, she thought about the conversation she had with Trisha and felt sorry that she had spent so much of her life trying to cover up someone else's mistakes. She wrote Trisha a letter too hoping that hearing from someone that none of this was her fault and that she shouldn't feel guilty would help her move past the whole situation and mend her relationship with Shannon. She then wrote a letter to Lily, thanking her for reaching out to her and helping her to mend her relationship with Cyndi.

Liz spent three hours writing letters and finally felt her heart beat calming down. She sealed all the letters in an envelope and put them in the eye lid shoe box Malik had made. She had a friend of hers buy it to encourage Malik to follow his dreams. She didn't want Malik to think she was buying it to make him feel good. She had truly been impressed with the work he did and wanted to see him succeed.

As Liz settled in for bed, she hoped that the next day would be a lot less eventful. She decided it was time to change her will. She had a lot more people that she cared about in her life and couldn't imagine not taking the time to leave a memory of how much she appreciated them.

A month later Liz sat in office of her attorney, Eli Whitley, for what seemed like two hours waiting to meet with him. She spent a few days deciding what she would do with her estate. She had never changed the will since the death of her daughter and realized that she had a lot of figuring out to do. The receptionist hung up the receiver at her desk and looked up at Liz.

"Mrs. Holden, Mr. Eli is ready to see you." Liz could feel her heart racing again. This time her fingers in her right hand started to tingle as well. She chalked it up to nervousness and walked into Mr. Whitley's office.

"Mrs. Holden, It's been a while. I'm glad you finally came to see me."

"Hi Eli, yes it has been. How are you?"

"Great, great. The practice is going well. My daughter got married a few years ago and I'm a grandfather now." Mr. Whitley's smile started to fade when he remembered that Liz's daughter had just died the last time he had seen her. "I'm so sorry. That was insensitive of me."

"No, it's fine. I'm glad to hear everything is going well." Liz forced a smile and slightly shook her head to shake off her tears.

"Well, I assume you want to update the assignment of your estate?"

"Yes, I've put it off long enough."

"I think five years is just the right amount of time to decide what you would like to do." Mr. Whitley grinned at Liz as he opened her file. "Let's see here. I have the latest copy the estate planning we've done. I'm going to go through this with you and we will discuss updates once I'm done."

"That's fine. I wrote down a few things that I would like to add but I think its best we go through the entire review first." Liz placed a letter on the desk in a white envelope and slid it toward Mr. Whitley.

"Ok. First on the list, the properties in D.C. and Georgia. These estates are currently assigned to Cynthia Holden. Do you want to change this?"

"Yes, I would like Cynthia to keep the property in D.C.."

"And the Georgia properties?"

"I would like one to be assigned to Malik Simms. I have his information in the letter I gave you."

"Are you sure about this Mrs. Holden."

"Yes, yes I am Eli. Please continue."

Mr. Whitley wrote notes on a notepad he had placed next to the documents from Liz's file. "Of course. Now, you have the Victoria Holden Foundation. The board is currently assigned to have the proceeds from the insurance policy distributed to General Hospital of Atlanta. Also, the board presidency seat will be transferred to Cynthia Holden." Mr. Holden looked over his glasses at Liz awaiting her response.

Liz could feel her hands clamming up. She gathered her composure and cleared her throat. "Yes, I still would like the policy to go to the hospital. I am electing Trisha Johnson as the president. She will run it from the Los Angeles office which will be the new headquarters for the foundation. Her information is in the letter as well."

"Are you alright Mrs. Holden? You look a little pale."

"I'm fine; I just have not been getting a lot of sleep lately. Please continue."

"Yes, as you wish."

"The only items remaining are the several stocks and bonds you have as well as your other liquid assets."

"I've written it all out in the letter." Liz said in a shaky voice. "May I have a glass of water please?"

"Yes, sure Mrs. Holden. And you're positive you're ok?" Eli asked with concern in his voice. He pushed the buzzer on his desk phone and asked his assistant to bring in some water.

Liz shook her head as she swallowed hard. She felt very warm as if she had a fever and slightly dizzy. She sat back in the chair and pulled a granola bar out of her bag. She hadn't eaten the past few days and figured she was just very hungry. The assistant brought the glass of water in and handed it to Liz. She started to feel a little better as she ate the granola bar.

"Before you go, please draft up a new will document for Mrs. Holden and bring it in for her to sign. She's not feeling well and I would rather not have to trouble her with coming back in the office later on this week to sign everything." He handed the file as well as the notes to his assistant. He then turned to Liz. "Do you mind waiting Mrs. Holden? She types quickly and it should take her no time to draft up the new will."

"Yes, I can wait."

"Good, in the mean time, I am ordering lunch. Let me get you something to eat please. Would a turkey sandwich be okay?""

"Oh thank you Eli that would be fine."

As they were eating their lunch, the assistant brought the updated documents in. Eli wiped his hands and looked through the documents for errors. He passed them over to Liz to review as well. "If they are in order, I just need you to sign where the red tabs are placed."

Liz looked through the documents and signed the proper lines. She smiled a sigh of relief as she handed the papers back to Eli. "I feel better already. Thank you so much Eli for seeing me at such a short notice. There has been so much going on and I was not sure when I would get another free moment before I left out the country again."

Eli nodded his head in agreement with Liz as he signed the documents on the witness lines. He stood up to escort Liz to the reception area. "Mrs. Holden, it's no problem at all. I have been working with your family for years. They're the reason I'm so successful today. If they had never given me so many referral clients, I might not have lasted two years at this practice. Listen, take care of yourself." Eli had a very serious look of concern on his face.

"I will Eli, I will. Thank you again." Liz smirked as she turned to walk out the office towards the elevators. She stopped in front of the elevator and pushed the down button. As she turned back around to waive good bye, she felt a sharp pain in her arm and then her chest. Her eyes rolled into the back of her head and she collapsed as the elevator doors opened.

Chapter Thirty

They all sat around the long conference table staring at one another. There were six people gathered in the conference room. Each person's name was written on a placard and placed in a strategic position at the table. They had received a letter in the mail two weeks prior requesting their attendance at a very important meeting. Some of the guests were confused as to why they had been chosen to be there and some afraid to speak to one another for fear of giving up information from their past. It was early afternoon on a Saturday in the middle of July. The sun was shining through the windows and generated an uncomfortable but bearable heat in the conference room. The silence was almost deafening as they waited for what they believed to be closure to a life they cherished and would never forget.

The sound of the conference room door opening broke the silence as the attorney entered the room and sat at the head of the table. "Good morning. My name is Eli Whitley. Your presence has been requested here today to hear the reading of the final will and testament of Elizabeth Holden. If you would all please acknowledge your presence once I call out your name. Darnell Allen?"

A brown skinned man with an Italian tailored grey suit gestured his finger in the air. "Yes, I am here" he stated in a stern tone.

"Gabrielle Santos?"

"I'm Gabrielle," stated a woman in a soft toned voice. She was seated beside Darnell Allen but had not looked at him from the moment she arrived.

"Trisha Johnson?"

"Yes, that's me" Trisha sat on the opposite side of the conference table across from Darnell and Gabrielle. Darnell stared with widened eyes at Trisha in awe. He had not seen her in over fifteen years and did not recognize her.

"Malik Simms?"

"I'm Malik" Malik sat on the other side of Darnell and like Gabrielle; he did not look or speak to Darnell Allen.

"Cynthia Holden?"

"Yes I'm here." Cynthia's eyes were bloodshot red. She had not slept the past few nights. She could not believe her sister was gone. She was angry and sad at the same time and being in a room full of people from her sisters past did not help. She knew why they were all here and that made her even more frustrated. As she looked around, there was one person whose presence calmed her down...

"Lily Woods?"

Lily sat next to Cynthia and Trisha. She reached out and placed her hand on top of Cynthia's. "Yes, I'm here." One tear fell out the corner of Cynthia's eye. She looked up at the ceiling to fight the rest of the tears that were developing in her eyelids. It hurt Lily so much to see Cynthia struggle with her sister's death.

"It looks like everyone is here" said Mr. Whitley. He opened up a folder that contained a small stack of envelopes and began reading the letter underneath of them. "Elizabeth requested I read this letter before we go on to the last will and testament."

The attorney opened up a business size white envelope and took a handwritten letter out of it. It had been sealed with the Elizabeth's signature, a purple butterfly. "And it reads as follows, 'Each of you at this table has a confession written by me on your behalf. I have placed these letters in a small chest in the secret compartment under my desk. You have two choices, you can allow your confession to be read aloud in the midst of the present parties or you can choose to take your confession and forfeit what I have left you in my will. If you do choose to have the letter read aloud, you must remain through the entire reading of the will or you will also forfeit your rights to any possessions left to you. The choice is your, but you must choose now.'" The attorney refolded the letter and placed it back in the envelope. "I took the liberty of bringing the chest in today." The attorney pointed to a beautiful hand-crafted lavender and gold chest that sat in the middle of the table. It was as long as a shoe box and had the distinct shape of an eyelid.

Malik shook his head in confusion. He had recognized the box but did not understand how it could've been the same box he had made ten years ago.

There was a thick cloud of tension developing in the room. Mr. Whitley stood up slowly and raised his left hand in the air. No one responded. They all seemed to be deep in thought. "I do have a few other appointments today. So, if you will all please take a moment and decide if you would like to remain for the reading of the will or forfeit your inheritance. If you choose to leave, please be sure to sign this waiver." He held a legal sized paper in his right hand, grabbed a pen off of the conference table and expressed, "This needs to be done now. Please understand that by signing this form, you are forfeiting your right of inheritance to Elizabeth's estate."

Darnell stood up in confusion. "I'm sorry but I'm still not sure why I'm here. How is it that a woman I hardly knew would have anything to say about me or anything to leave me?"

"Mr. Allen, I understand your confusion about this whole situation but I cannot say anything until I have consent from everyone to move forward." Mr. Whitley stated with a stern face.

"Well, let's make this easy for you. I don't want any gossip or lies told about me so I'll sign the waiver." Darnell walked over to Mr. Whitley. He picked up a pen, signed the waiver and waited for him to get the letter Liz had written to him.

"Anyone else?" Mr. Whitley asked as he handed Darnell his letter.

Everyone else sat quietly at the table as Darnell walked out the door. Malik was enraged about the way his father acted. He began to breathe heavily. Gabrielle got up from her seat and sat down next to Malik. She placed her hand over top of Malik and waited for him to look at her. They had not seen each other since the conversation they had at the cemetery.

Darnell was startled as he opened the door to the conference room and saw Danielle, Diane and David sitting in the lobby. They were seated next to another young woman who Darnell did not recognize. "What are yall doing here?"

"We got a letter to come here today for the will reading." David said.

"Well you're not staying. Let's go." Darnell reached out to grab his son's arm but David moved away from him.

"Dad, what's going on?" David asked in confusion.

Just then Eli walked out into the lobby. "You all may come in now. Thank you for your patience, there were some personal matters that had to be tended to."

David stood up and walked pass his father. His sisters, Danielle and Diane followed behind him, as well as the young woman that sat in the lobby with them. They all came in the conference room and sat in the empty seats around the conference table. Trisha looked with widened eyes and she began to slightly shake her head. She had not seen David, Danielle and Diane since they were babies. Tears began to develop in the corners of her eyes.

Darnell became even more confused at the presence of his children being at the will reading. He had a strong urge to go back into the conference room but his pride wouldn't let him do it. He pushed the button to the elevator and thought out loud, "Let the chips fall where they may."

Eli shut the conference room door and sat back down at the head of the table. "If no one else objects. I will begin reading the will."

Cynthia looked in confusion at Eli. "Wait a minute; I thought you said you were going to read each of our confessions first."

"That was the confession Ms. Holden."

"I'm confused Eli. Why would she say she's written a confession if she really didn't have one?"

"Ms. Holden, please let me finish."

Lily reached out and placed her hand on Cynthia's shoulder to calm her down. "I'm sorry Eli."

"Thank you. As I was saying if no one else objects, on to the will." Eli handed a personal letter to Cynthia, Gabrielle, Malik and Trisha. He then opened up the manila envelope and pulled out Elizabeth Holden's will.

"To my dear sister-in-law Cynthia, I leave the property located in Washington, D.C. with the stipulation that she utilize the house as a halfway home for women recovering from alcohol and drug abuse. I have also left a trust in your name for the amount of $25 million... I have assigned Lily Woods as the owner and Cynthia Holden as the trustee. Five percent of the trust is to be allocated for renovations of the property, twenty percent to be invested in stocks, and fifteen percent to pay off the outstanding debt of Ms. Lily Woods; with the balance of that portion going directly to Ms. Woods. The balance is to be given to Cynthia Holden in increments of five hundred thousand dollars every year she remains sober.

To Gabrielle I leave the deed to the property in Atlanta, Georgia. There is a safe deposit box in First Trust Bank that is to be assigned to you. It was your mother's safe deposit box. Inside you will find the documentation for a bank account that was set up in your name. I hope by this time I had the courage to read you the letter your mother left before she passed away. If not, I am sorry I left you to deal with this burden by yourself. You have a larger support system than you or I ever knew. Depend on them, they're your family.

Gabrielle's eyes widened and her heart raced. She had no idea what her godmother was talking about and became overwhelmed with the thought that she had family she didn't know about.

To Malik I leave the deed to the apartment building he lives in. This property was bought by me a year after you and Gabrielle began to live together. All of the rent you have been paying from that date forward had been placed in an escrow account. The account is in your name as the secondary owner.

To Trisha, I leave the position of president of the Victoria Holden Foundation. The headquarters will now be based out of Los Angeles, California. This foundation was created to help parent's of children who died from drunk driving accidents receive the proper counseling and legal assistance. With your law background and the degree of confidentiality you upheld throughout the years, I could think of no one better to take over the foundation.

To Lily Woods, I leave the ownership of the $25 million trust left for my sister, Cynthia Holden. I have also left twenty percent of fifteen percent of the trust to you to cover any debt you may have with the balance to be utilized as you see fit. Also, I have designated ten percent of the shares from the Victoria Holden Foundation to you. This will give you a seat on the board for this foundation.

The remainder of my assets, $22 million, are to be split evenly between Malik Simms, Gabrielle Santos, Zeta Dillon, Danielle Allen, Diane Allen and David Allen."

"I have just read in your hearing the will and testament for Elizabeth Holden. I am now handing out the envelopes that contain all of the information that pertains to the portion of the estate Elizabeth left for you." Eli stood up and handed the envelope to each person. When he arrived back at the front of the conference table he looked at each one of them as he spoke. "If you have any questions or need any help, please make an appointment with my assistant. Again, I am sorry for your loss. Mrs. Holden was a wonderful person and I was glad to know her as I'm sure you all were."

Chapter Thirty One

Lily was confused and overwhelmed at the same time. She did not think she made a significant enough impact on Liz for her to leave her anything in her will. Trisha was reading the letter Liz left her. Lily looked down at her letter and opened the envelope. She had to read it right then and there.

Lily,

First, I would like to thank you for helping Cyndi make this transition in her life. You have helped her in ways that I never could. I was envious in the beginning of how much she had changed without me. I spent years trying to convince her to stop drinking. Before my husband died, I promised him that I was going to do everything in my power to get her the help she needed. I didn't realize that meant letting her go. She has so much potential to positively affect so many people and the resources to do it as well.

To see how she has made such a dramatic change makes me happier than you could ever imagine and I'm sure my husband would feel the same way.

I truly believe because you choose not to alienate your faith in God from what you do, He's allowed you to affect and change people's lives. I include myself in that as well. You once said to me that you never had the opportunity to tell your brother he was forgiven. I believe everyday you spend helping those who are addicted to drugs and alcohol you're showing forgiveness. It takes a very compassionate person to do what you do and not judge the patients because of their short comings. I am truly grateful for what you've done in my life but especially in Cyndi's life. I could never repay you but I'll come close! I'm leaving in my will a percentage of money that should help you settle your debts. Also, there is funding that I will give to Cyndi and you to start up your rehab center out of the mansion in DC. I've left the property to Cyndi and since you guys have done such a great job at the rehab center where you met, I'm sure you'll do even better running your own.

We all fall short sometimes and don't think we deserve credit for things we do out of love. God's love covered your sins so that you could be forgiven. Some where in that process we are able to embrace that love and share it with others. That's what you've done and I'm sure you'll continue to be as affective to others."

Cyndi had placed her head in her arms on the table after Mr. Whitley had completed his reading of the will. She had begun to cry uncontrollably. She was confused and grateful at the same time that Liz thought enough about her to leave her anything in her will. Lily placed the letter she received from Liz down on the table and put her arm around Cynthia's shoulder. She tried to console her as best she could.

"It's going to be okay Cyndi. It's going to be ok.

"Did you say Cyndi as in Cynthia Holden?" The young woman that came in earlier asked in a foreign accent.

Cyndi lifted her head and wiped the tears from her eyes as she sniffled lightly. "Yes, that's my name. Who are you?"

"I'm your daughter. Zeta."

"My what!" Cynthia shook her head in disbelief. She was positive this was a hoax.

"I don't have any children." Cynthia said in a stern voice. She stood up, grabbed her papers and stormed out the door leaving Zeta sitting there in shock. Lily followed her out the door. Zeta remembered the name Liz had given her. She felt betrayed and wanted real answers. Zeta got up from her chair and walked out into the lobby of the office. When Zeta reached the lobby, she saw the doors of the elevator closing with Cyndi and Lily inside the elevator. Zeta tried to catch up to them but was too late.

Lily followed Cyndi to their rental car. She grabbed Cyndi's arm right before she reached the car. "Cyndi, you do have a child."

"Let me go Lily. Someone's trying to play a cruel joke on me. For all I know my child is dead. What makes her think I'm her mother anyway? How does she even know my name? I'll tell you how; Eli read it in the will. I need to go back to the hotel."

"Cyndi calm down please! Think about it, why would Liz leave money in her will for that woman if she didn't know who she was?"

"I don't know Lily and unfortunately I can't ask her." Cyndi started to cry again. "I need to get out of here!" Cyndi yelled at Lily.

Lily unlocked the car. Both she and Cyndi got in and they pulled off. "Will you at least read the letter Liz left you? There has to be something in it about this Zeta person. Why else would she be at the will reading. I mean she left her money Cyndi."

"I'll read the letter when I'm ready and right now the only thing I'm ready to do is sleep." Cyndi put her sunglasses on and closed her eyes. She couldn't help but notice how familiar the woman in the lawyers office looked to her mother. She erased the thought from her head as foolishness and rested until they were at the hotel.

"We're here Cyndi." Lily nudged Cyndi on the arm. She stopped the car in front of valet parking and got out. Lily walked around to the passenger side and knocked on the window. "Cyndi, we're here."

Cyndi got out the car and walked pass Lily without looking in her direction. She pushed the button for the elevator and waited for it to reach the lobby. Lily came and stood next to her. "You know Cyndi, this has got to be a lot for you to deal with all by yourself. You can talk to me about how you feel. I'm here for you."

The elevator doors opened. Cyndi and Lily got in and Cyndi took off her sunglasses to look at Lily. "Do you know what its like to loose the only person left in your life? I have no one, no one." Cyndi put her sunglasses back on and pushed the number 8 button on the elevator. Lily pushed the emergency stop button on the elevator and took Cyndi's glasses off her face.

"Yes I do know what it's like. I also know how it feels to never get to say good bye and never have the answer to questions that will plague you for the rest of your life. You had the opportunity to bury your sister. I wasn't given that chance. So, spare me the snide comments and remarks, I'm not the enemy here."

Cyndi took her glasses back from Lily and placed them on her face again. They did not speak to each other for the rest of the evening.

Chapter Thirty Two

Cyndi woke up the next morning hoping that she had been dreaming about the day before. She was still struggling with Liz being dead. To have some young woman walk up to her and tell her she was her daughter was almost too much. She grabbed her purse and decided to have breakfast in the hotel's restaurant. Cyndi got dressed and took the elevator to the lobby. As she walked towards the restaurant, she noticed the young woman from the will reading was in the lobby. Cyndi put her sunglasses on and walked past her as if she didn't recognize her. She requested to be seated in the far corner of the restaurant and sat with her back facing the entrance.

Cyndi enjoyed her breakfast by herself. She couldn't remember the last time she had actually sat down and ate breakfast. The waiter placed the bill on the corner of the table and Cyndi immediately reached in her bag to pay it. She fumbled through the bag for a few minutes for her wallet and realized she had taken it out the night before. As she pulled her hand out the bag, she saw the letter Liz wrote to her. She sighed very heavily and slowly opened the letter.

Cyndi,

If you only knew how many times I thought I failed you. It almost tore me apart when you started drinking when we were so young. I would get so upset every time we would go somewhere and you would completely embarrass me. In the beginning it was funny to me but as we got older and I saw that it only got worse, I thought that we had just grown apart. That was part of the reason I moved away. I judged you for something I never knew and now that I know, I will never be able to understand. I know I could never make up for what you went through and I would never want to try to. What I will try to do is show you the value in who you are and how strong you really are.

I took a trip to Portugal in August to visit Aunt Sara. I knew if anyone would have answers about your baby, she would. Your daughter's name is Zeta Dillon. Yes, you have a daughter! She is beautiful! She looks just like your mother. After she was born your cousin Alicia took her to nurse her. Because of the snow storm, the baby stayed with her until the doctor could get to the estate. She fell in love with your baby girl and couldn't fathom her going to a stranger so she raised her as her own. Zeta had no idea cousin Alicia wasn't her mother until I talked with Aunt Sara. Aunt Sara has no idea that Zeta knows who you are. I gave her a picture I had of you from a few years back. She would love to meet you when you're ready.

Cyndi, I know this is a lot to take in right now but you lost apart of your life over twenty years ago and I think it's time for you to get it back. I can imagine how you must feel right now but just know you're not alone. I'm praying that the anger and frustration you've bottled up all these years won't hold you back. You can change every pain into love and every heart ache into compassion. We've all fallen short at some point in our lives and no one but God has the strength to pick us up from where we are and guide us to where we should be. Your family did what they thought was best for you at that time and you can't change what's already happened. Take the strength that's inside of you and make the rest of your life the best of your life! I know you can do it, or I wouldn't have made that trip. Zeta holds inside of her a part of you that was taken away years ago. Help her to become what you couldn't. I love you and I can't wait to see the woman that you will become.

Liz

Cyndi placed the letter on the table and cried until she couldn't cry anymore. She had a daughter. More than that she met her daughter and didn't even know it. Cyndi wiped her eyes with the place napkin trying not to mess up her make up. She placed the letter back in her purse and put her sunglasses on her face to hide her red eyes. Cyndi took a long sip of water. A hand touched her shoulder and she remembered her wallet was in the hotel suite. When she turned around, Cyndi was surprised to see the woman from the lobby standing beside her.

"May I sit?" She asked.

"Yes Zeta, please sit." Cyndi said in a soft voice.

"So you know who I am?" There was a nervousness in her voice that brought more tears to Cyndi's eyes. She looked just like her mother. Cyndi shook her head as she took off her sunglasses. "Yes, I do. Liz left me a letter explaining everything. I'm not sure what you want from me. I haven't done much with my life to be proud of. In fact you being taken away from me might have been the best thing."

"Just tell me the truth" she said with her head down.

The waiter walked back over to pick up the check and asked Zeta if she would like anything. Cyndi grabbed the waiter's hand.

"I'm sorry, I left my wallet. Can you charge this to my room? It's room number 812."

The waiter shook his head in agreement and walked away with the check. She looked back at Zeta and grabbed her hand.

"If the truth is what you want, I can give it to you." Cyndi and Zeta got up from the table and walked pass the lobby to the elevators. Zeta pulled a photo out of her purse and showed it to

Cyndi. "Liz gave this to me when she came to see Grandma Sara in Portugal."

Cyndi looked at the picture of her self and shook her heard. It was from almost fifteen years ago right before her brother died.

"I've taken it with me everywhere I go. I hoped one day I'd meet the beautiful woman in this picture; my real mother. Wondering what I would say and what she would be like. " Zeta smiled as she spoke to Cyndi. The elevator doors opened and they both got in. She could not take her eyes off the picture for a fear of crying again. They reached the eighth floor and got off the elevator to her suite. "Why did you give me away?" Zeta asked in a shaky voice.

Cyndi stopped in front of her suite and turned to face Zeta. "I asked myself that every day." Cyndi opened the door to the room, turned the light on and sat on the love seat. Zeta grabbed the throw pillow off the side of the couch and sat down next to Cyndi.

"I don't get it then. Why were you in Portugal? Why not give birth in America?" Zeta said.

Cyndi could sense the tension in Zeta's voice. She placed her hand on top of Zeta's before she began speaking again. "I was raped by my father's best friend when I was fifteen. My parent's had a benefit gala at our house that spring and I guess he was too drunk to go home that night. He came into my room in the middle of the night and forced me to sleep with him. I was too embarrassed to say anything to my parents because he had told me I wanted it to happen. Truthfully I didn't and had I known what I knew now, I would've spoke up sooner. I found out I was pregnant a few months later and told my mother what happened. I don't think she believed me until she noticed how my father's best friend would look at me when ever he came over. When my father found out, he became furious and had him taken care of. I'm not sure of the details but I know there was a fountain built in the front of our house a few weeks later and has been there ever since. To keep the secret a secret, my mother called her sister in Portugal, Aunt Sara. She agreed to find a couple that would adopt the baby and made arrangements for me to stay in Portugal once I began to show that I was pregnant. I left during Christmas break and came back home some time in February." Cyndi sat back for a moment to collect her thoughts before she continued her story. She could see that Zeta was trying to take in as much of it as possible without becoming overwhelmed.

"I went into labor January 15th during a terrible snow storm. I was two months early but they could not stop my contractions and with the snow storm, no one could get in or out of the estate to take me to the hospital. My mother, your grandmother and Aunt Sara helped me deliver you in the cabin behind the estate." Cyndi paused again feeling the emotion swell up inside of her. Zeta placed her hand on top of Cyndi's and looked in her eyes.

"You don't have to tell me everything right now. We have the rest of our lives to catch up." Zeta gave Cyndi the softest smile she had ever seen. It melted the pain and anger she began to feel instantly.

"No, I want to finish. I've waited your whole life to do this." Cyndi wiped her eyes and cleared her throat. "I didn't get to hold you after you were born. Your grandmother, my mother, was afraid I would get attached to you and would want to keep you. I was so vulnerable and in shock about the whole situation that I just went along with what ever my mother said. Your grandmother helped me back to the house when I was strong enough to walk. I ran back out to the cabin a few hours later just to see you but you weren't there. I stayed in the bed for three days after that and barely ate. Like I said, we came home in February. I finished the school year out at home and went back to school in the fall. My mother tried to convince me that I would forget about you but I had this hole in my heart the day I lost you and I've had it ever since. I started drinking heavily at seventeen and tried to kill myself three times. I'm not telling you this for you to feel bad for me. I just need you to understand that I'm not the model person you may have expected me to be." Cyndi sighed and thought about how disappointing she must sound to Zeta. She had the intense feeling that she needed to tell her story to Zeta, her whole story. "I've done some pretty terrible things in my life Zeta but I'm proud to say as of next week I'll have been sober for two years. This is the longest I've gone without a drink and I've never felt more alive in my life!" Cyndi smiled at Zeta. She saw a peace in her eyes that made Cyndi feel like she had a reason to live. Even though Liz was gone, she had given Cyndi a reminder of what true love will do for you.

Chapter Thirty Three

Malik sat at the conference table in shock. He had no idea why Liz had left money to his brother and sister's. He could only imagine it was out of the kindness of her heart. As he sat shaking his head, David walked over to him. He placed his hand on Malik's shoulder which made Malik look up at him.

"We need to talk."

Malik could see the earnestness in his older brother's face and obliged with his request. Before Malik walked out of the conference room with his brother he looked back at Gabrielle.

"Are you ok?"

"She'll be fine Malik, we'll stay with her." Danielle said.

Trisha had begun to read the letter that Liz left for her but looked up when David and Malik left the room.

Trisha looked up at Gabrielle and saw how much she favored Danielle and Diane. The shocked look on her face scared all three of them. Trisha gathered her things and stood up.

"Excuse me Danielle, I'm sorry, I know you don't know me but I know who you are and I need to speak with your grandfather."

"I remember you Aunt Trish, it hasn't been that long. You can use my phone to call granddad. I'm sure he'll be happy to hear from you."

"Wow, I guess I haven't been gone for as long as I thought. Thanks for letting me use your phone. I will be right back." Trisha left the conference room and stepped into a vacant office next door to it.

"Bishop Allen, it's Trisha. I know, Danielle was at the will reading and she let me use her phone. I know it does seem odd but that's why I really need to speak you. No, it's not my husband and I, we're fine. It's about Darnell's daughter. No not the twins, his other daughter. I need to talk to you today. Do you have time for me to stop by? I know its short notice. Yes, thank you Bishop. I'll see you soon."

Malik walked into the lobby of the office and followed David to a few chairs that sat off to the side of the lobby.

"Malik, what I'm about to tell you might be hard for you to hear but since no one's mentioned anything about it to you before now, I think it's best you know."

"Ok, what? It can't be any worse than everything that's already happened in my life."

David sighed before he began to speak. "Dad had more kids than us."

"I know that Dave, he had me as well."

"I mean all of us. I think the girl that rushed out after that woman may have been our sister."

"What are you saying man?"

"I'm saying that there is a lot that I don't know and a lot that I'm sure you don't know about our dad. I think Aunt Trisha might be the answer."

"Who is Aunt Trisha?"

"I am." The woman who sat across from Malik in the conference room walked up to them.

"What is going on?" Malik felt confused and frustrated at the same time. He stood up from the lounge chair and placed his hands on his head.

"I was Shannon's best friend growing up. I also was Darnell's assistant when he was doing his crusades up and down the East Coast. David is right. You do have a sister."

"Well, do you know what her name is? I mean my sister, our sisters' name?"

"I'll explain everything this evening. Just meet me at your father's house. David, you Danielle and Diane should come as well. And Malik, bring Gabrielle with you but make sure both of you do not read the letter Liz left you yet."

Malik was completely confused but knew he needed answers and if it took a few hours to get them then so be it. He walked back into the conference room and walked over to Gabrielle. Danielle and Diane were sitting beside her on either side. He walked up behind her and placed his hand on her shoulder.

"We should go. I need you to come to my dad's house with me tonight."

"I just want to be left alone Malik."

"Well, unfortunately I'm not going to let you be alone

Darnell was too anxious not to read the letter Liz wrote him before he got home. Once he reached his car, he took the envelope out of his suit jacket and opened it. He began to read the letter as he sat in the front seat of his car.

Darnell,

I'm sure this will come as a shock to you but you changed my life twenty-five years ago. I went to a revival you preached at Ebenezer Baptist Church in Washington, DC. I was one of the fourteen souls that accepted Christ the last night of the revival. I had never experienced the power of God before that night and I truly believe that God sent you there if for no one else but for me. I want to thank you for allowing God to use you to be a vessel to reach out to lost souls. Out of everything I felt that evening, what affected me the most was what happened to my life over the next twenty-four years.

I was working in a strip club in DC as a bartender not because I couldn't get a job but because I was trying to prove a point to my future mother-in-law that I wasn't with her son for the money. It was pride more than anything that made me work there. I could've worked as an accountant at any firm in DC with my degree but I knew my mother-in-law would despise the fact that I worked at a strip club. Besides, my husband loved me regardless of what I did. He loved me for who I was, not what career choices I made. Had I never been so stubborn, I wouldn't have met my best friend, Lucida. She worked as a stripper at the same club and was one of the best strippers I'd ever seen if I must say so. (There's a purpose in me telling you all of this but I need to give you some background first.)

Lucida had met the love of her life, Hernando when she was sixteen but her life was not like mines. She grew up in a trailer home (like I did) but she didn't get the opportunity to get a scholarship to college like me. So, she chose another path to pay for her education, stripping. It paid her very well. While she stripped her way through school, Hernando worked as a foreman at a construction company outside of DC and took night classes to learn how to start his own contracting company. Everything was working out pretty well until Lucida got pregnant her last semester of classes. Lucida didn't know the name of her baby's father. She had slept with a man she met at the strip club and never even bothered to ask his name. Had I never been at that service that night, I would've convinced Lucida that having an abortion was the best thing for her. She was about to graduate and already had a job lined up once she became a RN. The love of her life was about to start a very lucrative career and there was no way he would be able to accept her having someone else's baby. But love prevailed, God's love that is.

You see, I had told Lucida and Hernando about Ebenezer Baptist Church and they began going to church with me. Hernando and Lucida accepted Christ as their personal savior and decided to start their life together, with their baby. Hernando loved her like she was his own child and she never knew or felt for one moment that he wasn't her father. Lucida died when their daughter was six and Hernando died when she was seventeen.

While this all seems like a lot, that's not the end. I moved back to Georgia and married the love of my life. I began attending church in Georgia and I also tried to convince my childhood best friend to attend as well. She suffered with serious drinking problems and I tried to convince her to change her life and live for Christ. I didn't realize she had deeper issues that she was running from. My husband died at the age of thirty-five and our daughter was killed in a terrible hit and run accident. Lily was eight years old, and the woman that killed her was not only her aunt and my sister-in-law but also my childhood friend. I was so devastated I took a gun and pointed it at her head. I told her I never wanted to speak to her again and had vowed I would never forgive her.

Bitterness and anger at God allowing so much misery and pain to come to my life in such a short period of time consumed my heart. I vowed I would never pray or speak His name again. My life was over, or so I thought! Like I mentioned earlier, my best friend Lucida died when her daughter was six, this was a year after I lost my husband and daughter. I had to return to Ebenezer Baptist Church to attend the funeral. When I walked in the doors of the church, I remembered the topic of the message you preached, "If This Is My End Then It's God's Beginning". I immediately felt that same feeling I felt when I first accepted Christ into my life. I remembered you talking about the man at the pool and how we could not judge whether what happened to him was because of him being cursed or because of a family curse. He had made a bed out of his issues instead of making crutches. I thought about all of the situations in my life that I had made a bed for me to lay in and die instead of using those situations as a stepping block so I could continue to move forward. Again, it was the word that God used you to plant in me that got me out of my rutt and reminded me of who God is.

I was blessed to find a ministry a few years later that helped me to develop a strong relationship with God. It was the building blocks I developed there that solidified my foundation in Christ. They also helped me to deal with what was yet to come in my life. Hernando, my God-daughter's father died when she was seventeen and became her sole guardian. She moved to Georgia with me and after high school she attended Clark University where she met a boy that saved her life, your son, Malik. She got into a bad car accident her freshman year of college that severely damaged her liver. Malik was the only match and agreed to donate a part of his liver. They were connected to each other in a way that could never separate them. As you know, their senior year of college Gabrielle got pregnant and had a miscarriage six months later. It was your father that held us all together through that time. I will be forever grateful for having a Pastor like Bishop Allen. Me writing all of this serves two purposes. The first is to let you know that Gabrielle Elizabeth Santos is your daughter. The second is that no matter how anointed we are or how involved we are in church, we've all fallen short of God's expectations of us at some point in our lives'. Because of this, I can't and won't judge you for your past. I would have to pretend I didn't make mistakes in my own life or attempt to compare your mistakes to mine. The same grace God had on you is the same grace He has for me, just a different measure. So, I only hope and pray that you take this opportunity to be the source of strength your family will need to get through such a terrible situation and be truthful about everything. Your family deserves the truth and it will set you free in the process.'

- Elizabeth Holden

Darnell sat in his car in complete shock. He had made so many inward changes in his life that he never thought of the outward effects of his past. He picked up his phone and called the only person he knew could help. He took a deep breath before he hit the send button. For a moment he prayed they wouldn't answer while the phone rang.

"Hello."

"Dad, I need to talk to you in person. I need your help."

"Yes, Darnell we definitely need to talk right now. Come to the house son."

"I'll be there in twenty minutes. I need to talk to mom too."

"We'll be waiting."

Darnell hung up the phone and for the first time ever, he felt fear take over his body. He pulled over on the side of the road and began to cry. He had changed his ways in the past because he got caught. He thought about all the people that had been and were being effected because he chose to bury his sins instead of exposing them and humbling himself.

Bishop Allen stood in the door way of the house as he saw Darnell's car pull in the driveway. Darnell noticed his wife's car and a car he didn't recognize was already in the driveway. He took a deep breath and prepared for what would be a long evening.

"Come on in son. Shannon's hear and so is a long lost friend."

"Dad, I don't think we should have anyone other than family around for what I'm about to say."

"Trust me son this is family."

"Hi Darnell." Trisha came out from the family room and stood in front of Darnell.

"Trish, I'm sorry I didn't get to speak to you after the will reading. I…"

"No need Darnell, we have bigger issues to deal with."

"So you know about Gabrielle?" Darnell asked both Trisha and her father.

"We all know." Shannon said as she came out of the family room as well. I've known for years, I just couldn't fathom it was the same Gabrielle. Darnell, Jesus! Did you think you could go through life forgetting you ever had a past?" Shannon was now yelling with tears in her eyes.

Bishop Allen walked over to Shannon and placed his hand on her shoulder in a comforting way. He looked at Shannon with deep intense eyes. "We all need to talk this through before we talk to the children."

'Dad, no, I'm going to deal with this by myself. I'm stepping down as pastor and I'm just gonna come clean about my past to the kids. This mess I got us all in has been going on long enough. I started this whole mess and I'm going to fix it."

"No, Darnell, you're not stepping down. You're going to be a man and address this straight on and deal with the repercussions as they come. The reality is, the past is the past. We are a family this is our situation to deal with, not just yours. We're all going to sit down and talk this through. That has been your problem. You truly believe that you don't need to rely on anyone to help you and it's mainly my fault. I allowed things to go on and just prayed that you would change before things got worse. But you're not God Darnell. You don't have the power to fix everything, not on your own. Now lets all sit down and work this out. You can have a pity party later but right now your family needs you."

A few hours later, David, Danielle, Diane, Malik and Gabrielle all arrived at Bishop Allen's house. They looked confused to see Darnell sitting in the family room with blood shot eyes.

"Dad, are you alright?" David asked in a concerned voice.

"He's fine. Please come and sit down, all of you." Shannon said.

Darnell took a deep sigh and looked at each of his children as they sat together in the room. "We should pray." Darnell said, as he reached out for his wife's hand. "Dad, can you lead us in prayer?"

Bishop Allen stood and grabbed his wife's and Malik's hand in the circle. "Heavenly Father, we are grateful for your loving kindness and tender mercy that are new every morning. We thank you for yet another day that we all have the opportunity to show you how much we love you and appreciate not just what you've done for us but who you are. We ask that you touch the heart of each person gathered here. Help us to come together as a family and support one another at such a tough time. Give us the strength to make it through this situation and help us to gain understanding as to your purpose behind this situation. We need to wrap your loving arms around us and heal all wounds, past and present Lord. You are our source of strength, our rock and our redeemer. We're nothing without you and if you were to take your hand of mercy off of us we would be lost. We love Lord and bless your Holy name. Amen."

FROM THE DESK OF DR. HAYWARD R. HAMILTON

One Can Never Escape Themselves....

The futility of secrets has a vast impact which may result in closure, healing and resolve or resort to means of long-lasting negativity and pain. We were created to implement God's love and grace to all that we embrace and become ensamples of the same as we live. As we mature in God, our selfish nature dies and comes to the solemn understanding that we are absolutely nothing without God! Peradventure, while this is a prevailing truth, we become more dependent upon our OWN strength and wills because we have, in our own judgment, overcome so much. This leads to lives of vain controversy that strip the innocence from the walls of life, and force mankind to envelope themselves in the whimsical paradigm of double lives. This life may not resemble their present status but it grows into a defense called unforgiveness that cast light on others when the God through someone else dimmed the lights (forgiveness) in their favor to be restored.

Whether it takes the anatomy of unforgiveness or act of suicide because of guilt, they are both characteristics of the enemy called: SELF-RIGHTEOUSNESS! Firstly, the ability to forgive is housed in the heart of one who has been forgiven and resolves the details in their own heart. Pointedly, if one has been forgiven, they must undoubtedly forgive themselves to master forgiving others. A major debilitation of forgiveness is when one has not thoroughly been healed or lack of understanding of what they have done negatively, themselves. True deliverance sets the stage for pure forgiveness. Secondly, in a world where all things are made accessible and corruptness is not seemingly forbidden, the continued surrender to a higher power is a requirement to avoid becoming an undesirable. Alternately, when one walks the path of what they didn't plan, they oft times chose to become the God of their own lives by either suicide or self-harm. These two emanate from fear, shame, and pride. This form of self-righteousness has a costly end.

1 Corinthians 10:13 (KJV)

There hath no temptation taken you but such as is **common** to **man**: but God is faithful, who will not suffer you to be tempted above that ye are able; but will with the temptation also make a way to escape, that ye may be able to bear it.

Therefore, as we live, we must walk in humility as to never become untouchable with reality, but at the same time not become a slave to it. As we age, we will be challenged; however, age does not equal maturity. With this being established, venture to never humiliate yourself and frustrate your purpose by bowing to challenges in your latter years that were easier to overcome in there Genesis. The hills of challenges do not have to become mountains. What you feel you failed at may be someone else's deliverance. Your surroundings play a major role in ensuring that any imperfection, undesirable item of your past, and short-comings are channeled properly in effort to lessen the torture. While there is no one around us that is perfect, there is a perfect love:

1 John 4:17-19 (NIV)

[17]This is how love is made complete among us so that we will have confidence on the Day of Judgment: In this world we are like Jesus.

[18] There is no fear in love. But perfect love drives out fear, because fear has to do with punishment. The one who fears is not made perfect in love.

[19] We love because he first loved us.

As **L.A. Lambert** has successfully navigated us through the arduous waters of the human experience, the foundational truth but yet layered principal of restoration protrudes. Everyday we come short of man's expectations, are own goals and God's divine will. Our true mission is to consider ourselves and move closer to perfection by moving further away from vain judgments.

Galatians 6 (KJV)

[1]Brethren, if a man be overtaken in a fault, ye which are spiritual, restore such a one in the spirit of meekness; considering thyself, lest thou also be tempted.

[2]Bear ye one another's burdens, and so fulfill the law of Christ.

[3]For if a man think himself to be something, when he is nothing, he deceiveth himself.

You are your own worst enemy but today can become your greatest asset to awareness. An awareness that you need integral people in your life; an awareness that no one is perfect but perfection can forever be attained; and an awareness that we are absolutely nothing without the acknowledgement of our Creator. Who you were to become is never that far away that restoration can not redeem the time remaining to still pursue. Live will live without you; so never let its mobility out run your success. Pull yourself out of the abyss of guilt and move ahead. Closely monitor every decision made, because it will inevitably impact your tomorrow and someone else's future. In closing, I leave with a word from our sponsor, God or Father:

Joel 2:25-26 (KJV)

[25]And I will restore to you the years that the locust hath eaten, the cankerworm, and the caterpillar, and the palmerworm, my great army which I sent among you.

[26]And ye shall eat in plenty, and be satisfied, and praise the name of the LORD your God that hath dealt wondrously with you: and my people shall never be ashamed.

At this point you might be wondering why I decided to end the book this way. It is because we always focus on what we would do if we were on the outside looking in on someone else's life. I asked my Spiritual Father and Mentor to comment on the spiritual aspect of forgiveness because this is significant at any level of restoration. I wanted you, the reader to experience the various different dynamics of exposure, or "shedding of light". It was important to make it understood that there is no cookie cut reason as to why someone lies, cheats, steals etc, but there is one common enemy to changing this from a present action, to a past memory. That enemy is judgment. The Bible talks about the redemption of man and being justified by God's grace. What is the most significant part of the third chapter of Romans is verse twenty three, "For all have sinned, and come short of the glory of God." We sometimes forget that even though we may not have been a cheater or an alcoholic or an adulterer, we were something. We may revert to having a snobbish attitude or a condescending tone we give to people who now do what we use to do. The reality is, whatever we use to be has either been hidden inside something else or covered by us becoming so sanctified that it's not even prevalent that we had a past. Either way, it is an act of sin that separates us from being God and sometimes also separates us from getting close to God.

I focused on both of these aspects in the book and tied them in with the significance of light. It is important to understand that while you're condemning someone for their down fall, or for hiding their light under a bed, your other sense, hearing, is deafened by what you see. If we take the time to listen to what someone says, we may gain a better understanding of why they are that way or what caused them to become what they are. It is this understanding that will help us have a greater compassion to people who may not act, think or look like us. If we do not gain this understanding, we could be holding someone back from making a change in their life because of the fear of unprotected exposure.

We all fall short of what we are supposed to be at one point in our life. The significance is, what will you do when you fall short? Will you try to hide what you've done so no one will know and therefore they can't judge you? Will you condemn others for their wrongdoings to keep the focus off of you? Will you use what you made it through as a testament to how gracious God is and to encourage someone else? The choice is yours but you must choose wisely because you may be forfeiting the inheritance or reward for being a living testament.

www.ingramcontent.com/pod-product-compliance
Lightning Source LLC
Chambersburg PA
CBHW030328020726
47493CB00004B/1202